THE DINER
DOWN THE ROAD

Nathan Twiss

authorHOUSE®

AuthorHouse™
1663 Liberty Drive
Bloomington, IN 47403
www.authorhouse.com
Phone: 833-262-8899

This is a work of fiction. All of the characters, names, incidents,
organizations, and dialogue in this novel are either the products
of the author's imagination or are used fictitiously.

Published by AuthorHouse 12/29/2021

ISBN: 978-1-6655-4813-7 (sc)
ISBN: 978-1-6655-4818-2 (e)

Print information available on the last page.

CHAPTER 1

WAKE UP JOSH

The story starts in the small town of Glue Bend, North Dakota which was found to be in the middle of nowhere. In a raggedy old duplex on the east side of town which was just 2 miles away from the North Dakota and Montana border. It was the early morning when I was fast asleep when my wife woke me up. I woke up to hear her saying "Josh Josh wake the hell up! Why is it so hard for you?"

When I finally decided to open my eyes I saw the clock and said fuck not again it was 8:15 AM I had fifteen minutes before I needed to be at work. I reluctantly got out of bed and got ready for work. I worked as a cook at a local diner it was famous for its chicken pot pie that for some stupid reason my boss put hot sauce in.

His name was Denver. He was this short 5 foot 2 gentleman with black hair in his 50's with a sweet wife named Debra. But more on them later.

Back in reality I was naked standing in my bathroom, as I was trying to figure out how the hell the shower faucet worked as it had just been installed 2 days ago. I was so used to the old one that I just had no clue how it worked as I fidgeted with the faucet handle it finally turned on and seeing that I was running low on time it didn't matter that the water was frigid. I then started washing myself, getting rid of all the bed sweat from the night before. Soon I was done. I then stumbled out of the shower and frantically tossed my clothes on and kissed my wife, Jazz. She was a tall brown haired blue-eyed woman with a smile as big as the sun. We released our embrace. I then ran out the door, hopped in the car and raced away almost recklessly.

CHAPTER 2

THE STRANGE PANHANDLER

As I was nearing work I got stopped at a red light. Wondering what had caused the light to change I looked up and saw an Arabian Woman holding a sign that said "My husband lost his job. anything helps."

I had just been paid and had plenty of money to spare so I pulled a 20 out of my wallet, rolled down my window and stretched my arm out the window and handed it to her. The light turned green and I sped off. As I did I thought to myself,

"What is an Arabian family doing in a middle of nowhere town if they came to America for opportunity. They sure as hell wouldn't come here. They should have gone to a big city with more jobs, not this old run down town with nothing to do." All we had in this God forsaken town was an old ass roller rink that doubled as a bowling alley, a run down grocery store, the few hotels, and the bank down the road from the Diner on 2nd Street, and of course Denver's Dinner where I

worked along with the huge highschool where almost every kid in the county went.

In addition to that the racial diversity was super uneven; it was 95 percent White and 5 percent African plus there wasn't any Arabian culture that this Woman and her family could latch onto. We were really just a bunch of white people who worked 9 to 5 jobs. It left me puzzled. But anyway, I went on with my day as I was already late for work.

Chapter 3

The Ruined Griddle

As I entered work, Denver exclaimed "There you are my friend" in his normal outgoing tone. Denver wasn't bothered that I was late. He turned and said "Start prepping that chicken" which happened to be 20 feet down the cook line. He had already taken the supplies out of the cooler for me as he did all the time because I was always running a little bit late to work, but my work ethic in turn made up for my tardiness. I walked my way down to the line and washed my hands. As I finished, I turned to grab a towel. To my surprise another hand had beat me there. It was Ray, my best friend since 12th grade.

The year I moved to Glue Bend I moved from Stockton, California where I was born and raised and I was the only white kid in my neighborhood. That is the very place where my dad got shot while watering my mom's roses. After that my mom was terrified of the neighborhood and had been begging my dad to move out of that place for years. So as soon as the funeral was over she sat me down at the table and told me we had to move in with my grandparents. With dad gone we simply didn't have the means to pay the bills, so two months later we filled up the moving van and made the trip to Glue Bend.

While I wasn't the cool kid in school by any means, it was where I met Ray, a cool down to earth, weed smoking, sport playing, black kid from Phoenix, Arizona. We were both new and so it just worked. We were kings on the football field both playing on defense and Ray also played Running Back which he dominated.

I remember it was the first game of our senior year and it was 3rd and 6 and Ray got a hand-off and almost in a blur he was running down the sideline. On the other hand he also played on Defense with me. I played middle linebacker, and he played cornerback. We ended up losing in the Semi-finals to the next county Overs Hoover Bobcats. Now five years later, I had just graduated from colunary school, which was stupid to do because it got me knowere but working at a dinner for 13.25 an hour. Ray was fresh off a Narcolepsy diagnosis, which cut his college football career short. I guess he had suffered too many concussions and it messed him up badly that now he would fall asleep all the time randomly. So he moved back in with his Mom and I got him a job at Denver's Diner.

It was destined to be a busy day because on Fridays pot

pies were 16 inch instead of 10 for the same price of $15. So, Ray and I hurried up to our stations and got to work. He was knocking out pie crust and vegetables, while I was cutting up chicken and monitoring the sauce. The sauce contained brown sugar mashed cauliflower, jalapeno seeds, 1 oz of broccoli water, 1 oz of tomato juice, a half an ounce of lemon juice, a half an ounce of lime juice and 4 oz of buffalo sauce with a little bit of rice mixed in it. Talk about a weird concoction, but it made a hell of a good pot pie that sold like butter. After about 45 minutes we had about 200 pies ready to go. So we placed them in the cooler for later that night. From there we would get ready for the morning rush.

Soon we are making omelets by the 20 and pan cakes by the hundreds. After about 2 hours it slowed down but the damage was done. Batter caked the wall, egg shells glued to my apron, and Ray turned to me with a concerned look on his face looking down at the griddle. He had forgotten that he had placed the batter spoon on the edge of it before the shift had began and now it's plastic handle was melted to the $3000 industrial griddle. He began to panic, saying "Shit, I have to drop out of college now, I'm going to get fired from 1 out of only 10 jobs in this God forsaken town. I laughed and said, "Chill man. I'll go get Denver. He can help." Just as I turned, there was Zoey, one of our hosts. She glanced over, began to chuckle, and looked at Ray and said "You pulled a Josh. He then glanced at her and said "What are you talking about?" I turned towards him and smiled and said in a breathless hysterical way, "Yeah, it was like my 5th day and I did the same thing. I almost quit out of pure shame, but Denver just laughed at me and said just scrub it with a old spatula and wire brush and it comes off like no big deal.

So we grabbed the wire brush and after about 10 minutes of scrubbing, it was finally off. Denver came in the back and said "I heard what happened and looked at me and said, "Well done, you've trained him well." He had a silly expression on his face. Then the room burst out in laughter. The remainder of the shift was pretty chill. A few cheese burgers here and there and the occasional breakfast burrito.

Since it was so slow, Ray and I blared our music, singing alone to some Logic and Kanye and even some Neil Diamond just because. Denver had gotten sick of not being able to keep up with the lyrics. We laughed at him saying, "Nah, you're just deaf. We all laughed, but Denver only haphazardly. Then we got back to work. The day was going by quickly and it was around 6:00 quitting time. Ray and I bumped knuckles and said, "See ya later," as he headed toward the back door. Ray said, "Wait, I got 2 extra tickets to tonight's game. My mom and sister were going to go with me but they decided to have a girls night out. Would you and Jazz wanna tag along? I said, "Sure, I'll see you there in 45," as I rang out a rag I had been using to wipe down the prep area down with. I then put back my supplies and clocked out. I Picked up Jazz and we were off to the game.

Chapter 4

Remembering The Good Old Days

Before I tell you about how the football game went. I have to give you my back story. You already know some things about me. Like how I grew up in Stockton, California. And how my dad died and so on.

Well to tell you more about him. He was a man with vibrato but very kind. He was a car salesman and my mom had a paper route. They were highschool sweethearts graduating in 1995 married in 96 and had me in 1997 I was a home birth crazy as it sounds but the reason was because the doctors at the hospital sucked and she couldn't trust my life in those hands plus her mother was a nurse so it felt more comfortable for the whole family. And now I have a bomb story to tell my friends. But anyway I was 6 pounds 2 ounces with black hair and hazel eyes.

I grew up always watching sports with my dad. He was

my best friend. He always taught me a lot. I learned more from him than from school. Teaching me how to rhyme, and he was the reason I ended up going to culinary school because we would always be cooking all types of foods from chicken to stir fry and every kind of grilled food you could think of. It was always a good time.

I remember on one occasion we were cooking chicken fried steak and my dad accidentally poured a whole container of salt in the pan. We both laughed and said to ourselves well this will be interesting. Later when We ate it with my mother she gagged and started hitting him with a newspaper thinking that he had pulled a practical joke on her.

His cooking always seemed to bring the neighborhood together too. As he would invite all the neighbors over for a Cookout and we would have an amazing time. Playing basketball in the driveway and football in the street. Matter of fact my dad was grilling the day he died and when the authorities left, I walked in the backyard to a burnt to charr piece of chicken.

That was the hardest day of my life. After my dad died I was depressed. It took months of me just sitting in my room playing GTA and binge watching Netflix. It wasn't until I met Ray and when he convinced me to try out for Football and that dude along with my grandparents who I hadn't seen since 5th grade who moved after I turned 10 comforted me through the toughest part of my life.

My Grandpa was the best. We would watch College

Hockey together and he really did his best to take the place of my dad. He showed up in every moment that mattered. when I broke up with my first girlfriend he was there. When there was a new movie coming out and Ray was busy my grandpa would pick me up and we would drive 20 minutes to the next town just to watch some silly movie. He took me to Church on Sunday and sat front row when I was baptized.

My mom was also very endearing even though she was very sad she always stepped up and put a smile on her face. It was the most heart wrenching moment on senior night. Me, her and Grandpa walked across the field tears dripping from her eyes just knowing how proud my father would have been. As he was my flag football coach growing up and how much joy it would have brought to him. Those were my mother's words after the game.

Between my mother Carly, Grandpa Luke and Ray they got me through so much. But most of all my Wife is the person who changed my life the most. Towards the end of highschool I met my wife. She was working at the roller rink when one day I came in and complimented her on her eyes just as a kind gesture. The next time I was there she gave me her number. We were just friends for a while but after 6 months of talking she got tired of it and asked me out herself and the rest is history.

CHAPTER 5

THE GAME

It was the second quarter tied 17-17 as we saw Phil. He was one of Ray and I's coworkers, he did prep on Saturday and Sunday on his days off from the bowling alley. He was a tall stubby man with thick calves, a bold head and had a long salt and pepper goatee. He had a deep raspy voice and was very loud. Phil was in his late 40's and had 4 kids 2 of which played on the football team as he sat down next to us he yelled ''Go get it Connor'' which was his son the ball had just been fumbled as Connor dived for it from his defensive tackle position. Everyone erupted as he recovered the ball at the 30 yard line giving our team great field position.

On the very next play the quarterback threw a missile through the middle of the Field right into his tight end's reach for the touchdown. They then lined up for the extra point and the kick was good. The referee blew his whistle it was half time. I looked over to Jazz and asked her if she wanted anything from the concession stand. She shook her head. I then glanced to my right and said" Ray what a great half" and to my dismay he had dozed off. I shook him and said "Ray come on wake up brother" as I laughed a little. He shook into consciousness and drowsily said "huh what's up"?. I said dude you're missing a good game man then proceeded to ask him if he would like anything. He nodded and said some cola would be great.

I turned around and walked my way down the old Medal stands down to this shack-like building which held all types of food. This nice lady greeted me saying "Josh Pokks is that you.?" I said yes. She said "It's really nice to see you. She was one of my old teammates, mom's Greg Johnson. I said yep that's me. She then asked well what would you like. I looked around and pointed at some chips up on one of those clips that you see at the Supermarket that holds miscellaneous things like cheap toys and such. Then I asked for two cola's. She nodded and handed me the food then said that it would be 7 bucks. I gave her a 10 and said keep the change.

I then walked up to the first row of the bleachers and watched the marching band for the next few minutes as they played Their own version of Thunderstruck. Once the performance was wrapping up I headed back to my seat. I handed the soda to Ray who was again almost asleep. I was always worried that he would fall asleep at the wrong place at the wrong time. I then popped open my bag of chips and settled in for what was for sure going to be a good second half of football.

The other team was returning the second half kick-off. Our kicker put the ball on the tee backed up then signaled his guys to run. Then booted a bomb. It landed at the 10 yard line where a big husky full back picked it up. The blocks were set and he had a hole the size of a semi truck to run through. He looked up and ran. He cut up the field and booked it for the end zone which he made it to. Tying the game. That score would be the last that they would have. From that point on Glue bend took full momentum. I guess maybe they got pissed off and started scoring touchdowns one after another.

By the end of the game it was 74-24, an absolute shalacing by The glue Bend Rockets. As the game ended the crowd roared. Everyone in attendance knew they had just watched a team poised to be in the same place as me and Ray were just 5 years ago playing for a state Championship. Our group stood up. I shook Ray's hand and thanked him for the tickets and gave a nod to Phil and his wife then placed my hand in Jazzes and headed toward the exit. After a lot of shuffling through the crowd we made it to our car and headed home.

I opened the door and so tired from the long work week and long night I didn't even bother to get undressed or even head to my room but instead just crashed right into the couch Jazz did the same but she didn't fall asleep right away she picked up her favorite book and finished the chapter she was on. After that she kissed me on the forehead and cuddled up next to me throwing a blanket over both of us.

Chapter 6

A Flood For The Ages

At this point a few weeks had gone by and the diner was busy as ever and now Denver had just given me a small raise. The football team had just improved their record to 3-0 and it was super rainy outside. It was about three o'clock on a Tuesday afternoon. Me and Ray had just gotten done organizing the walk in which we never had time for other than today. Because of the rain most people were staying inside.

So Denver said he would watch the kitchen while we cleaned everything. Phil had just showed up to work his rare Tuesday shift that he would work if the bowling alley was slow. He was bagging fry's so we wouldn't have to weigh them out when a rush would come.

Almost out of nowhere we heard a pound coming from outside and along with it a high pitched screech. We all looked around asking each other what in the world that could be. A few seconds went by and we heard a car alarm going off in the back of the loading dock. I opened the door and there was about 2 feet of water quite literally rushing into the restaurant and I then glanced further ahead and saw Zoey's and someone else's car crashed into the dumpster. I was mind blown. I turned to Phil and said now how in the hell could you have made it here with this much water. He laughed and said in his deep and proud voice when you have a lifted diesel truck it isn't a problem. I then said oh that's right.

I then yelled hey Denver "tell Zoey her car is currently floating in trash". She was just around the corner and yelled wait what do you mean I parked that thing on the hill because I knew this parking lot might flood. I said well it's not there now. She pushed me out of the way and started lunging towards her car. I followed after her to see what had happened to her car as we got closer I could see that her fender was smashed under the tire and the rim had unshaped itself into an oval-like shape. I then jokingly said we know a thing or two because we've seen a thing or two like that guy from those insurance commercials.

She looked over at me and said shut up Josh I only have liability on this thing I'm screwed. I said well I'll call you a tow truck. So I did. She clocked out and sat in the diner waiting. I then called Jazz to make sure she was ok. She informed me that our neighbors had been kind enough to put sandbags around the house but my shed was a bit flooded. I shrugged and said it will dry out. It only contained a tool box some golf clubs and my old football pads. I talked with her for a few minutes then said I love you and hung up.

I looked around at the flood damage zoning out a little bit. Then I heard Denver yell from inside hey buddy were calling it a day man go home. I clocked out. And ran to my car. Knowing there was no way I could make it all the way home I parked it on the hill and asked for a ride from Phil. He obliged.

As we rode along we saw this little girl who had fallen in a ditch and was struggling in the current. Phil slammed on the brakes throwing me forward in my seat then flung me back in my seat. We then proceeded to exit the car and rushed toward her. Phil grabbed her arms and I grabbed her by the torso. We lifted her into the car. She was gasping from the adrenaline rush she was experiencing. We asked her name and age. She said Gem, that's my name and I'm 11. Phil then asked Randy's daughter right. She said yes. I asked, "What were you doing out here?" She said "I was standing in my yard when all of a sudden the fence broke and swept me away." "I've been out here for a while." We both said "well you're safe now". Phil called her dad and took her to the hospital where her dad was waiting and then took me home. I got inside Jazz had also just got home from the store and had her paycheck in hand we unlocked the door and shuffled in and slammed it behind us.

She had a smile on her face. I asked her why she said "you're so handsome when you're soaked in water". I then said "well I'm also kinda sexy when I save little girls from drowning too". She gasps and says, ``Really, what do you mean"? I then told her what had happened. She was amazed. She also was discussed that I was covered in mud. She pointed to the shower and said "now go". She kissed me on the cheek and said "oh and I have a surprise for you when you get out". I turned and looked at her suspiciously. She smiled and gave me a smirk.

I got in the shower and cleaned up. I got out and shaved my face and wrapped a towel around my waist. When I exited the shower. I then called out for Jazz. She said "I'm in the bedroom".

I entered the room to see my wife unclothed with a bottle of wine in her hand. I asked, ``What is this all about". She said "well we never got to properly celebrate your raise". I said "well ok then as I grabbed a glass she had poured for me and was now handing it to me. She kissed me as she pulled the towel off my body. Took the glass from my hand and set it on the night stand then pulled me in close and began to kiss my neck and rub my shoulders.

We made sweet love that night and when we were done we drank a little and watched a few movies as the storm died down.

Chapter 7

The Day I Had To Serve

The day started as it usually did. I got up early this time, fiddled with the shower and freshened up. Shaved. Kissed my wife and walked outside. I looked to my left and saw that the patio furniture had tumbled over from the storm the night before so I picked it up and strained it up. I then turned towards my Car which wasn't there. I had forgotten about how I left it at work the day before. So I said to hell with it I'll just walk.

It was only a 20 minute stretch so I got on my way as I walked. I saw David who was my neighbor. He said quite a Storm right. I said there's never been any truer words. I nodded and went on my way. I walked through town and as I passed the grocery store I said to myself an energy drink and a donut would be great right about now. So I turned around and made my way across the parking lot and on into the store. I then made my way into the bakery side of the store and grabbed a box of glazed donuts and then made my way to the registers. I noticed just how dim the lighting was in the store given the storm and how the store was over 50 years old with hardly any renovations even had those fake wood looking freezers and such. But anyway I got to the registers and grabbed my drink from one of the little fridges that they have then set it on the conveyor belt. I then greeted Mrs. Wessons who was running the register, a nice old lady in her early 60's with short dyed red hair. I paid for my items and then walked outside. I popped open my drink and downed half of it like a boss. And then I pulled it from my face and gasped to catch my breath.

After that I walked about another quarter of a mile to work. As I walked into work I saw Helen, one of the servers. I asked her how her morning was. She then said "I feel terrible". I was taken aback for a second and then replied "well I hope you feel better". Then Shrugged. I turned the corner and saw Denver. He saw me and said hey Josh we gotta talk. I said "well alright what about". He pointed to his office and motioned me toward it.

We sat down and he said I have some news for you buddy. I said well what would that be. His head was down it seemed as though something terrible had happened he then looked up and said we only have two serves today. I said yeah oh really just Helen and well who else. He then said and you. I said well who's going to cook? Rays only been here barely a month wouldn't that be super overwhelming. He then chuckled and said and that's why you're going to do both. I then shook my head and said well I guess today's going to be a long day.

We stood up and exited the office we heard a loud burp and what sounded like spaghetti hitting the floor which as odd as Denver's diner didn't serve that. A split second later it occurred to me that someone had just vomited and as I turned to look out onto the dining room I saw a huge splat of puke on the table and Helen was bent over gasping for air. Denver rushed over to help her. I stood there and just looked up to the ceiling and said really God and then shook my head. Ray then came behind me and said shit today gonna be crazy. I murmured oh you don't even know. He patted me on the back and said hey at least it's not Friday. I smirked and said you better not fall asleep back there today. He jokingly said oh fuck off.

The day was just about to start. I grabbed a pin and a ticket book and walked into the dining area that had about 25 tables, and 30 booths with big glass panels that split each booth and there was a large waiting area where there were about 30 people waiting to be seated It was go time.

I ran over to them and started seating as many people as possible. Taking orders and then rushing back and forth from kitchen to diner non stop for my whole shift. If you could imagine a montage of someone writing an order down and then seeing a pan with food in it. That was the perfect screen. The day was hell. It happened to be the best grossing day in Denver's diner history

Which I found hilarious. As my shift winded down Denver pulled me aside and congratulated me on my efforts and then handed me $200 dollars that was on top of the 13.30 an hour I was making and $75 dollars in tips I had made. Though I was wiped out, the day was pretty awesome.

I walked away with 300 dollars. I clocked out and walked outside and lunged up the muddy hill where my car had been sitting for the last day. I got in my car and zoomed home. What a day.

Chapter 8

The New Sign

I had been working for an hour when I heard a knock on the back door. So I placed my spatula on the grill and went and opened it. There were two middle aged men standing there holding a large box. One holding it as if he was going to drop it on his foot. The other man said well are you going to move? My buddy here is about to break his toe. So I backed up and shuffled to the side and as they swiveled their way on into the doorway I asked what was in the box. And one of the men said you're gonna like it, it's the new sign.

I said that's cool. Are you guys installing it too? As they put the box down one said nope just dropping it off but I do pity the people who will have to lift this thing 10 feet in the air. They then shook my hand and went on their way. Me being curious took a box cutter and sliced the tape that was sealing it shut. I flipped open the flaps and looked inside to see a big red and orange sign that said Denver's diner in this really cool acrylic font and it had a certain shine to it like a new paint job on a car. I was in awe.

I looked up and saw Denver standing over the box with a smile on his face. He then said this place is about to get an upgrade. He then grabbed a ladder and said come with me kid the restaurant is slow and I need some help. I then pushed the box to the front. Thinking to myself why me. We got outside and set up the ladder. Denver pointed at the box and said you got me. We started lifting it up and just as the sign was reaching the roof Denver's hand slipped and it tipped and fell right on his foot. He fell down and yelled "oh God" writhing in pain. I grabbed my phone and called 911. I took it from my ear and looked down at my phone. It was dead. I instantly panicked. And got jittery. Denver yelled "Josh go get Debra she can call". So I jumped out of my daze and ran inside when I got inside Zoey said "what the hell is going on out there". I replied Denver just broke his foot call 911". She pulled out her phone and called.

A few minutes went by and the ambulance came and Debra guided her husband into the back of it. I felt responsible, head in my hands she looked over to me and said it's okay son you did what you could. The day went on awkwardly everyone was sad knowing our adeered boss had just badly hurt himself.

I got off and clocked out and as I walked outside Ray invited me over for drinks but I said nah it's ok man maybe some other time. I made my way to my car, hopped in and put my key in the ignition and turned it expecting it to start to no avail. I pounded my hand on the wheel yelling could this day get any worse. Then the airbag exploded in my face. I shook my head, opened my door and said hey Ray I'll take those drinks after all.

Chapter 9

The New Hire

A couple days had passed and my car was stuck in the shop. So I was getting rides from Ray. About 3 days in he told me that he overheard that there was going to be a new guy working in the kitchen doing prep. I said oh really what about Phil. He replied well Phil only works a few days a week and with the diner being so busy we're always running low on hamburger meat and such and now we wouldn't have to make the pies as the new guy would take over that job we would just have to throw it in the oven. I looked over to him and said well that's a relief.

Inside I was actually excited to meet the fellow. We pulled up to the diner and walked inside. We saw this young kid, maybe 20 years old or so, talking to Debra. He was very tall, had light brown hair, almost blonde, had a scruffy beard and walked with a limp. He looked our way and gave us a smile and put his hand out to shake mine. He said hey guys my name is Martin I'm going to be your guyses prep cook. I smiled back and said my name is Josh and this is Ray pointing one hand to Ray and putting out the other to meet his hand. Debra glanced over our way saying now that y'all have met you can train him Ray I'm going to help you on the line and Josh you take the day to help this kid find his way.

I turned to Martin and said tell me about yourself as I was showing him how to use the slicer. He said well I moved here from California when I was one and pretty much have been here since. I asked him if he had any siblings. He said oh yeah a brother but one day he left and we haven't seen him much since says he's living in Montana somewhere working on some ranch. He then told me how he had just gotten married to this sweet Irish woman of the same age. I said well congratulations and told him how I got married soon after highschool as well. I then asked him why he limped. He told me that somehow he had a stroke before he was even born and showed me his brace that he wore and also his hand which was a little under developed and weak.

We talked and worked for an hour or so and then I showed him how to portion different things. We did that for a while until the rush started then I told him I had to hit the grill. He said I got this. So I ran over to the grill and started whipping out food. We turned on some music and got going.

About an hour later Martin asked if he could have the aux I reluctantly said "sure hoping he wasn't gonna play some weird dubstep". I was pleasantly surprised to hear a

Rapper I had never heard of streaming flows together Bar after Bar. I looked up nodding my head to the music and asked who this is. He laughed and confidently said that's me. I bumped his knuckles and said you sure got talent. 6 o'clock came around and so I clocked out and me and Ray got into the car as we were about to leave. Martin ran over and handed us a CD and said that's my mixtape. I said "wow thanks man". And popped it into the Rays CD player and waved goodbye to my new friend. I got home watched some college football with my wife and hit the hay wondering what tomorrow Would bring.

CHAPTER 10

THESE ARE THE MOMENTS THAT CHANGE YOUR LIFE PART 1

The next few days went by with few notable moments. And then Sunday September 25th came a day that will forever stay in my mind. I walked outside to see my Car finally fixed. The battery had gone out and the radiator was rusted and after 2 weeks of being in the shop 20 miles out of town it was fixed and ran like new.

I lifted my Key from my pocket and in my other hand was a shopping list that Jazz had made for me. Chocked full of all types of supplies for the next 2 weeks of meals. It had steak, rice, potatoes, Cheese, and bread amongst a million other things. As I looked at it I said well this is going to be a long day.

Jazz usually liked doing most of the shopping since she was the desk lady at the hotel that was only about a block away. But on this particular day she was very tired and felt sick to her stomach. So me being the endearing husband I am, I decided that I would do it. So I hopped in the car and drove the way towards the Store.

When I got there I started to scooped out the place trying to remember where everything was. As I did a large elderly man ran into me with his shoulder and his kart rammed into mine. He just walked on by. Me being a little irritated I said what the hell man no I'm sorry young man or nothing. The man who looked familiar looked back at me and said now son is that anyway to speak to your Grandpa as he chuckled. My expression changed and I smiled and said oh hey Grandpa how are you doing it's been awhile. He said yeah I hear you've taken a lot of responsibility at work given silly old Denver dropped that damn sign on his foot. I said yeah poor guys gonna be a few weeks before he can even come back to work with a boot on. We both laughed a little bit. Then he looked at me and said well where's that wife of yours?"

I said to him she's super sick at home so now I have the duties of trying to find all these groceries. He then said "and you don't know where a damn thing is"? I got shy and said yeah not much at all. He said well then I'll help you. He started walking as I stood there a little confused still in my head trying to figure out where things might be. He turned back and said well son are you coming with me or are you going to wander around here like a lost dog. I then shook out of my daze and followed behind. He pointed out where the pasta was and said you need some.

I looked at my list and found it towards the bottom and then shook my head saying yep. We went down the aisle and grabbed some angel hair and spicy sauce. We then headed to the snack aisle where the peanut butter and jelly also were. My grandpa grabbed a glass jar of jelly and turned to put it in the cart. He seemed off, his eyes were glassy and he seemed jittery. He looked up and said help me, grandson. Then dropped the jar on the ground, shattering it. Then in an instant fell. I screamed for somebody to help my grandpa.

CHAPTER 11

PART 2

I stood there as time seemed to freeze. I felt like a poison. Denver and now my own grandfather. I kneeled with a heavy heart, my mind now racing wondering if the emt would make it before he would meet his fate as he lay there motionless. I looked down and shook my head. Moments later the emt was there and they were pulling me off of his hip. Everything went black. When I regained consciousness there was a man motioning me to enter an ambulance. My sight and hearing cleared up and he said sir would you like to come with us. I said oh yes. And then stepped into the cab.

After about 3 minutes my grandfather was waking up asking me what had happened. I told him you passed out but you're going to be just fine. But in my heart I just knew it was far more complicated than that. A minute or so passed and we were at the hospital. They led us to a room and hooked my grandpa up to an IV and gave me some water. They ran all types of tests to no avail. An hour had passed and grandpas and my phone both rang. It was Jazz. I picked up the phone and explained what had happened. She was shocked and said I'll get down there with mom and grandma. I cut her off and said I'm pretty sure grandma is on her way.

About 20 minutes went by and everyone was huddled in this small emergency room. And the doctor entered and said well we haven't found anything yet. Grandma looked up and said well what do you mean by yet. The doctor said well I was hoping we wouldn't have to run this last test. Grandpa who was pretty out of it and had been quiet for the duration of his time said in a heavy gravelly tone well doc what are you saying. The doctor cleared his throat and said we got to test for Multiple myeloma and then posed. I looked over and said hell sir what is that.

He sighed and said that means Cancer. He may have collapsed from sudden pain and when he fell his hairline fractured his arm. I looked around the room and everyone was blank and completely expressionless. And then all the sudden Jazz just barfed all over. The doctor said oh dear and then turned to the nurse who was in the other room and said can you prepare a bed she seems sick to. The test was going to take 90 minutes to come back from the lab so I decided to stay with jazz. She explained to the doctor how she was feeling very sick for weeks. Nauseous and with no energy always tired, hungry and dehydrated and it's been sensitive down there. They ran a few tests. It wasn't the flu, or any weird diseases and the doctor then handed her a piss test. I said she doesn't do drugs or anything. He glanced at me and said she might have a UTI. She was out of the room heading towards the bathroom. He then sat me down and said did she have her period? I said well it's late sometimes as it is this month. He smiled and said she's either got a UTI or you're going to be a Dad.

He then smiled and put his hand on my shoulder and said I think it's the ladder, congratulations young man. And walked out of the room. 5 minutes went by and sure enough he was right, me and Jazz held hands and then both started crying with mixed feelings of joy while in the back of our minds we wondered whether this beautiful child would ever meet it's great grandfather. We heard a loud scream from next door. It was my mother and grandmother. The doctor had just given them the news and then I heard my grandma say 2 to 8 months are you serious. She then entered our room and hit the ground. I put down the pregnancy test and huddled with her as the rest of the family joined in. I tried to comfort everyone but it was useless. Then we heard from the inside of grandpa's room to hell with me. I'm 78 years old and what's wrong with that poor girl. Everyone paused. I looked up and yelled hey grandpa you're getting old you're gonna have a great grandbaby. Almost in an instant the somberness turned to an out roar of cheers and laughs.

There was a Young boy in the room next door. He yelled you people are weird one minute y'all are crying the next you guys are laughing and cheering. The boy's mom said excuse him and congratulations and also said I'll be praying for your grandfather.

Chapter 12

Amir

The next few weeks went by as almost as uneventful as possible. I was pretty gloomy given what was going on with my grandpa but I was extremely joyful to be bringing a Child into this world. Denver's foot had finally healed. Ray got promoted to shift manager and found himself a sweet little curly haired girlfriend. The football team was 7 and 0. Jazz had her first ultrasound and we found out she was about 10 weeks along and looking back we had conceived the day of the flood when Jazz surprised me. Grandpa found out that the cancer was stage 4. I guess one soul leaves for the other to come or something like that.

Martin was also settling in really well and making a good name for himself and got one of his songs on the radio and landed himself a gig at the bowling alley. It was just a laid back shift when Debra asked me to take the trash out. I grabbed the bags and went outside as I made my way to the dumpster. I suddenly heard a scrum in the parking lot.

4 football players were beating up this young kid. He was maybe 14 or 15 with dark black hair and we looked Arabian. I yelled hey Stop. I started to run towards them.

They were yelling get your mother fuckin tarists family out of this country we gonna fuck you up especially after what your brother said he would bomb the school. As I got closer the kids scrambled away cussing and yelling. As the scene cleared I looked down and said hey kid you okay dude. He said oh just more of the same. It's like this every day for me. It's my brothers and dad. They are always talking crap about American and how you guys are such awful people and are

Always trying to ruin our way of life. I swear they take their beliefs a little bit too seriously. I said yeah sounds like it. That one kid said your brother wants to bomb the school is that true. The kid said nah he's full of shit always saying stuff like that but never backs it up. I said "well my name's Joshua what's yours kid".

He put his hand out and said my name is Amir, unsure if he was supposed to shake my hand or not. I smiled and shook his hand. I shook my head and said well Amir let's get you cleaned up. I took him inside and Debra cleaned him up. We tried to get the cops involved but given it was 4 football players bullying a Aribian kid they probably bullshitted the report. After the Cops left I told him to stick around and after I finished my shift I would buy him some dinner and give him a ride.

He in a skeptical tone said well I guess so. I finished my shift and found him in a booth. I sat down and said well kid when did you come to America. He looked up and said oh about 2 years ago. I looked up and said "what does your dad do for work?" He said oh just odd jobs and he also helps break colts out in Montana. I said oh that's cool. I told him how I had seen his mom on the road a few months ago.

I then told him about myself and we ordered some food and cracked jokes. He killed the food in minutes. I asked him "do you need some food?" He said no and then said "can you take me home now". I said "I guess so". We got in the car and made our way to his house.

As we got close he told me to stop the car. I said why kid, we are right around the corner. He then looked over and in an honest tone said if my dad sees me with you it will just be bad news. I pulled the car over and said well Amir nice to meet you and said if you need me I'll be at the diner Saturday Monday Wednesday Friday and then wrote my phone number down on a piece of cardboard. I then drove off and went on home. I had really taken a liking to him and knew he needed a friend.

Chapter 13

The next day was a very good day. It was a Friday everyone was leaving town to go watch our beloved highschool football team win their last game of the season which would give them the first seed in the playoffs. It was a very close game through the first half. The score was 7-6 Fort Yates. Then as the second half went by. The Glue Bend Rockets started chipping away and the defense of Glue Bend started slamming the door.

They ended up beating Fort Yates high school 23-7 and everyone was so happy until the mayor got a frightening call. Someone had set the outskirts of town on fire and the Williams farm had been completely burnt down and one of the hotels had been broken into. I wondered to myself who would have done such a thing or why we wondered if the fire was an act of arson or just an accident. I couldn't figure it out. I looked over to Ray and Jazz and Phil and said why exactly would someone burn down the outskirts of town and break into a hotel for it just didn't make sense. We are in the middle of nowhere. It confused me why would someone do that to their own town.

When we got back to town we saw that there were a lot of things misplaced. It was kind of odd like someone I just came in and tore the place up. It was almost like when you leave two teenagers at home alone and they get in a fight in which the whole house is torn up, that was our town or at least the outskirts of it. We didn't even have a dedicated police force in town so the surrounding counties investigated and found that the fire wasn't arson or so they thought they at least thought they couldn't figure anything out in the break-in to the hotel it was just some petty thieves just some missing food from the snack bar and some missing printer paper.

It all felt so odd though who were those Petty thieves there was so many people at the football game that night before that it almost seemed like our whole town was there I was confused our Town had over 2,000 people and I thought I'd seen just about everybody at that game it was such a big game so whoever done that crime knew that no one would catch them. Like it was almost planned in advance. But anyway life went on no one really thought it was all that bad it seemed it as they figured well there was a storm rolling through that night before maybe some lightning struck a tree the night before and there was a small fire brewing while we weren't there and that's why there was a fire and most of us figured someone just wanted to steal some cash from the hotel and couldn't find their objective so settled for second best. No one seemed to really care but I knew inside of me something was wrong but I kept my cool and just went on with my life knowing in the back of my mind that something weird might happen, something that we didn't have any preparation for.

A couple nights later I was at the restaurant making preparations for the next night's elementary School fundraiser. We would sell pies like usual and half the profits would go towards the elementary school's playground. It was a long night not going to lie. I stayed there until 12:00 a.m. I was the last one there. I locked up for the night and went on my way as I left. I saw a dark shadow and I wondered, huh that's kind of odd so I shyly investigated when I peeked around the corner I saw amir I said kid what are you doing out so late. He said oh just wanted to talk to you. I said well that's kind of weird, but I guess you can.

He went on to tell me that he felt that something really weird was happening in the town and he was scared he'd been living there for about 6 months he said and it seems so common now people kind of looked at them funny and that the kids at school were beating up on them every day and his brother was getting really irate with people more than usual. He told me that his brother's threats were even more deep, cutting and terrifying. I asked him "what is your brother saying"? He told me that he thinks he might be planning a terrorist attack. I said wait what you must be kidding me what is he going to do. The kid replied to me saying I think he's going to go shoot up some cattle and set a house on fire. I said well what house and where. He replied beats me he just keeps saying weird stuff like that and he's going to go shoot some stuff up and do some crazy stuff to some people out of anger or something he says that the Quran says that if people aren't going to conform to what it's saying that we should kill them I always grew up to that notion that that's how it should be but I've been seeing lately that a lot of people are just good people and they didn't grow up like me and they don't have the same values and that's okay that's why America is supposed to be a free country. But when I tell that to my dad or my brothers they beat me not too bad I guess they just are so into their beliefs that they don't know any better.

He then said to me but I don't think they'll do anything at the end of the day, they're kind-hearted people. I told him well you keep me up to date with this stuff and if you know that someone in your family actually will act out on something like this to tell me. I then ask them why do you come out so late at night to tell me something like this. He then looked up at me and said well if I were to do this broad day everyone would know and they would blame me for it as the cycle would continue.

The whole situation to me felt kind of unsettling but I knew one thing: this kid needed somebody to listen to him and to influence him in a positive way. So I looked at them and said well I'll see you later, you can always talk to me. The next day the fundraiser came around. I was super busy that day cooking all types of pies and trying to make sure the oven to get overfilled with them me and Ray were real stressed but the elementary school made over $50,000 that day and we knew in just a few days the Denver would be back with a good clear bill of health we were all excited about it we haven't seen our boss in weeks he finally been out of that boot he was in for all that time and he finally back in action even though you've been back a little bit he'd really be back. And he was just in time for the county fair one of the busiest times of the year is after the fair. Everyone would come in and stay there until the next morning as we didn't close till 2:00 a.m. It was always a meeting place for everybody just to enjoy themselves after big events.

CHAPTER 14

It was nearing Winter when I was driving to work one day when I saw a bunch of cattle loose walking across the road that had me confused there was in cattle for like 3 miles out of town the way the town was shaped was there were about 4 MI circles and there's three of them that made like this triangle shape and on the outside of those triangles there were usually small farms some of which were now burnt down from the fire and it would take forever for a lot of those cows to go wandering into town especially right in the middle of town where I was.

So me being peculiar I pulled off to the side of the road and got out of the car I looked around really confused. Being a little bit frightened I decided well she probably come please so that's what I did. One of the police officers was about 15 minutes later pulled out to my site and said now this is kind of weird. We've got that fire then we've got the hotel being broken into and now cows wandering through town like it's freaking cars the movie. I said yeah isn't it really odd you said well something we can really do about it but figure out where they came from and return them to their owner there are about 15 of them gathering now. The police officer walked up to one of the cows to see if you had a brand on it. The brand was a a j with a cross through it. That meant that it belonged to Jason Tayr; he was one of the cattle owners in the next town over. We both looked at each other and said no way his form was like 10 miles away from here. I knew that because some was always getting bussed to school and would wait at the diner for his dad after school and I was always making food for him. But anyway the police officer who told me I'll take care of this looks like you were heading to work if you hear anything tell me and he gave me his card. I politely nodded and went on my way thinking to myself what is all this mischief adding up to. Did these cows just break a fence and wander 10 miles away from where they belonged? That would be a hell of a coincidence but I almost felt like something really weird was going on. When I got to work it was a calm presence over the place.

It was 8:30 in the morning and the place that just opened and it wasn't one of our busier days. I headed to the back and I saw Denver and I smiled and said I'm really glad to see you back man we've been missing you a lot it's been hell to keep up with everything around here. He laughed and gave me a nod. He said well Josh you did a real good job and then said I got a good job for you son we're going to help Martin portion everything today. I said well that sounds like fun actually so I headed to the freezer and grabbed a few different supplies and menu items from there and headed to the station. I flipped through the storage rack and grabbed a scale and a portioning box and went to work. A few moments went by and Martin was standing next to me. He smiled and said I got some good news. I said well what would that be. He said "I got a gig to play a few songs at the bowling alley next weekend". I was wondering if you wanted to come. I said that would be great. We could go to the fair and then I'd give him a ride afterwards. He said "that would be great if we could have a double date or something dude". I said that sounds perfect I'll bring my wife you bring yours go to the fair then when it gets to be around the time that your show is going to be we'll just head right in. He said that the show started at 7:45 and now we should head to the fair at 2:30 and leave around 7:00. I said it sounds like a plan dude.

We got to work knocking out about 10 boxes of fries and six boxes of onion rings that day. Right before the day was over I looked over to him and said hey I would like to invite you and your wife to eat dinner with me and Mine. He nodded. "That sounds like a good plan". I'll see what I can do. He then said "we've been struggling to buy groceries so it would really help if we had a good home cooked meal so I'll tell my wife". I looked over and said "I remember those days it was a bunch of TV dinners, cheap generic sodas and discount store bread". He said "yeah sounds about right". As we both headed out we said goodbye to Ray he said "yeah you guys go along now i'll be here till 12:00 prep for tomorrow see you guys in the morning". Me and Martin gave him a fist bump, clocked out and went on our way.

Later that night Martin and his wife came to our house. We sat around the dinner table talking about life. He told me how his grandpa passed in 2012 from bone cancer. That's when I told him my grandpa was on his way out too. He assured me that it will be really hard for a while and then you start forgetting about how hard it is and start remembering that you can still make him proud. He told me how at his Grandpa's funeral he was only 9 years old and he stepped up to the podium and said everything I do from this point on is for my grandpa. He told me how he loved playing baseball in those days and how he said every base hit, every stolen base, every home run, every strikeout was going to be for his grandpa. It really gave me perspective how that young of an age 9 or 10 years old this kid really knew that he loved his grandpa that it really mattered to him that he was making proud even when he was gone.

He told me how he and his wife met each other online and how she lived in Canada for a long time but decided to move to North Dakota to be with him and how they got married on New Year's Eve just the year before. I told him about me and my wife's honeymoon. It was literally just going to her hotel that she worked at and staying in the nicest room. We all laughed and said well that ain't so bad we still had plenty of fun and we got away from reality for a little bit.

The conversation went on for an hour or so then we decided that we should watch a movie. We ended up watching a Clint Eastwood movie, a real old one too, one from like the 70s when he was in his prime. After the movie finished, we hung out for a couple more minutes and then looked up at the clock and it was already 11:00. Martin said oh we got work tomorrow we should get going you guys have a beautiful night. As Martin and his wife left they congratulated us on our pregnancy and promised they would try to buy some things for the baby. We smiled and said no way we got it taken care of guys you guys worry about you. I was really happy to know that I was gaining friends that could really be there for the rest of my life. As you know in high school that really isn't the thing you go to school with those people and you see them at parties and stuff like that but now I was gaining these friendships that would never end. That I had someone that had so much in common with someone that understood me like Martin did and that Ray did and that both of them would go to bat for me for the rest of my life be good friends to me and I would do the same for them.

Chapter 15

When Hell Freezes Over

It was about 6:00 in the morning when I got a call on my cell phone. I was tired from the night before watching a movie late at night and having dinner with my friends so I let it ring thinking to myself who would be calling me this early in the morning. I looked up and saw that it was Denver's phone number and thought he may have been wanting me to come in this early today. So I called him back. He sounded a little bit frightened as he said you should come down here right now son. I said why it's so early I'm not scheduled till 8:30 he said trust me son just do it, no questions asked. Me thinking I had done something wrong said okay sir then I hung up the phone. I grunted and said all right Jazz I'll see you later. Then I went to the bathroom and put some deodorant on and brushed my teeth, grabbed the cheese stick out of the fridge, and then walked outside and forgot that I was still in my underwear and it was 40 degrees outside. So I headed back inside and grabbed my clothes through them on my way.

As I pulled up to the diner I saw an ambulance and a few cop cars. I wondered to myself what mischief is going on now given the cows, the fire outside of town and the hotel and now did someone break into the diner and steal some bread and hamburgers I laughed at myself. As I walked up to the back door I saw Denver. He had a stone look on his face like something absolutely terrifying had just happened. I said dude what's going on why did you call me in so early. He glanced at me and said nothing. I spoke up again and said "common buddy, what happened here"? He muttered and then pointed "just go look" as his head pointed towards the ground. I walked inside the diner and saw that there were a few police officers huddling around the freezer. I asked one of them what happened here. Did someone steal something? They all looked over and put their hands to their faces. One looked up and then looked over at his partner and said should we let him see. The other police officer said "I guess so this is his best friend". I said "who's best friend"? Another police officer looked up at me and said Ray froze in this freezer last night. He fell asleep sitting on a little stool that is in here and just didn't wake up. He's gone. A terrified expression went over my face as I raced towards the freezer pushing both of them out of the way I looked in. There was Ray hunched over lips purple and his eyes were frozen shut. His hair was turned into icicles. His phone was still in his hand. I shook my head and started weeping. I looked over at the cop and said he had narcolepsy. That means he falls asleep at random times and random places and you can't do anything about it and if people don't watch out for him he'll fall asleep in places like this and never wake up again. And the unthinkable happened. I felt to my knees breathless. The guy that got me through my senior year, the guy that I had played football with the Brother I never had that gave me a purpose to even live to the end of my high school years that got me through my dad's death the guy that put a smile on my face every single day of my life since I was 17 was sitting frozen to death inside a freezer and I couldn't do anything about it.

My best friend was gone. I thought to myself the worst is yet to come. Ray dies now and my grandpa's going to die in a few months and I thought to myself where do I go from here as pain and anger rushed through my body.

The next few days it went by. I felt like I was in a daze the whole town was morning. Ray was a legend; he's the only football player to ever go D1 from this town. So naturally everybody knew who he was, everyone remembered the accomplishments that he had on that football field and for the people like me that actually knew him outside of those walls we were all broken, especially me I actually wish I wouldn't have walked into that freezer it had scarred me for life.

After about 2 weeks his mother had finally been able to put a funeral together. We all gathered at one of the local churches just outside of town many people gave their eulogies. They were cookie cutter as most of them didn't really know him that well. But when it was time for mine I had some deep thoughts that I needed to pour out of my head. I looked up at the crowd and said

"Ray was my best friend. He was literally the only person
in my life that could give me hope when I was lost in
my journey in life. We both moved here the year of our
senior year his mama had just divorced his dad and he was
going through a lot and me I just moved from Stockton
California and my dad had just been shot there just a
month before we were both going through hell he knew
he wasn't going to see his dad much anymore and for me
I was never going to see my dad again. So natrually we
strengthen each other we were both super depressed but
we knew we had to do something about it he decided
that the only way he could get his anger out was on that
football field and he decided to ask me to join him me
knowing that I was still depressed as I ever had been so
knew I had to do something so I joined him it was my last
ditch effort if it didn't help me break free it would have
been taking my own life instead. Rays Friendship saved
my life. And with that our bond began to really really
strengthen through those 5 months. Family's got close. I
got close with his siblings and they became my family.
I remember when he went off to college it was the day
before he was going to leave and we decided to sit down

and have dinner and shoot the shit he told me that man
you got me through a lot dude and will never ever leave
each other's side. I remember us watching film that
night too and I told him when you go down there to
Iowa State you best bet you score some touchdowns for
me and he said touchdowns more like championships.
He would call me every weekend right after the game
and asked me did you watch I said yep you guys played
good or when you would lose I said your team didn't
play good but you did and we both would laugh and
he tried to defend his team saying well it's not like
we're playing easy competition playing Oklahoma isn't
so easy you know what I mean. And then I looked up
to the crowd again and said we also work together.
I remember it's always making pies for the diner for
you guys out in this crowd. I trained him too there
was nothing like that being able to show your best
friend how to make a pie it seems so miniscule but
It actually mattered to us Ray always took pride in
whatever he did he knew he wasn't going to play football
after his injuries so making those pies and flipping
those burgers and everything that went along with
working in that diner was very serious to him and he
was working his way up Denver told me that he might
become a manager one day if he's stuck with it"
    I started crying and said Ray tala may you rest in peace
and then walked off that stage full of sorrow.

CHAPTER 16

YOU CALL THAT A PROPER RESPONSE

A few days went by and I was still in my stupor. Until Jazz told me hey Martin's wife called and wondered if you guys still wanted to go to the fair. I looked up at her and said well I am kind of sick of just sitting in this room. I guess I'll go but I'm not going to be that happy. She said well I can understand where you're coming from maybe it will help you out. I said I guess I'll go.

So a few hours went by and it was time to go. Martin called and said he would meet us there. I said No no it would waste gas for both of us and Martin to drive there in two different cars me and Jazz decide we would pick him and his wife up. When we pulled up to their house I was shocked.

There was a shack-like structure only about 600 square feet but I knew that's exactly where I had been just a few years earlier before we were able to buy our small hat house. The house was painted tan with a black trim. And no garage and a few broken windows. I didn't judge though. Martin and his wife came outside and waved. Jazz rolled her window down and unlocked one of the doors. Martin's wife looked up at us and said how are you guys doing. Jazz politely said I'm doing okay but Josh could really use a pick-me-up right now. Martin then said well that's exactly what we're going to do. They both climbed in the car and Then I started the car, pulled out of the driveway and made our way to the fair.

As we pulled up to the fair We saw big blinking green and red lights glaring off the car window they were coming from the ferris wheel that was about 45 feet tall. This made me tear up a little it reminded me of when me and Ray got kicked out of the fair for rocking the seat on that very Farris wheel just 2 years ago. I looked over to my Wife and said he's everywhere as I put my head down. she shook her head and said who's everywhere. I looked up and said in a choked up manner Ray. I started sobbing uncontrollably now. Every memory started rushing in.

Even the stupidest things like signing each other's yearbooks. I thought the grief was wearing off but I was entirely wrong. I sat there in the most sorrowful moment of my life as what I was aware of in my mind finally was intriguing my soul. I sat there motionless. Shaking my head in disbelief. The whole Car was now huddling around me, every one patting my back like you do to a newborn when it is upset. Time seemed to stop. It was like one of those scenes in a movie when the camera and you just observe overhead.

Eventually I began to chuckell and said Fuck it Ray would be on the Farris wheel trying to flip it upside down then I pushed the roof of the car and yelled let's goo. Everyone laughed and yelled let's get it. We than got out of the Car and strolled towards the gates. When we got there, who was standing there none other than Mrs. Johnson had a sweet smile on her face with her flowing burnet hair. She nodded and said how many I said 4 ma'am. That will be $12. Martin stepped in front of me and handed her a $20.

I said why buddy. He stopped in his tracks and said because you've been a great friend. I looked in his eyes and said well you have been to. We then headed towards the Carnival foods. We all ordered Corn on the Cob and then headed to the music stages. There was an old man playing Cover songs by Neil Young and such. We listened to a few songs. Then headed for the rides. We got to the ticket booth. I told the man I'll take 4 passes. Jazz who was staring at her phone, looked up and said I can't, I'm pregnant, can't go on any rides silly. Then Martin's wife giggled a little and nervously said make it only 2 Martin glanced over and said well why Kelli. She then reached into her pocket and revealed a pregnancy test with two lines reading positive. Martin froze and then smiled and began to tear up full of joy. They embraced both giggling as Martin placed his hands on her stomach. Me and Jazz looked at each other and said now what a coincidence. We then joined them in joyfulness. Jazz hugged Kelli and I shook Martins hand and said you ready he looked back and said well are you and we both laughed. I then said well it would be rude to of us to ride without our wives he agreed and we looked over to the ticket man who was nervous because a line was starting to form. He said well would you like anything. Me and Martin seamlessly said nowhere good.

We then walked with our wives back to the music stage. We spent about 4 hours listening to music. There was a Jazz band. A highschool Metal band that thank God only had a four song set as we were ready to just up and leave as it sounded like the lead singer was in the process of coughing up a lung. After that there were a few country singers and even a Comedian.

At about 5 o'clock we round up our things and headed to Martin's gig at the bowling alley which he said would be 10 times better than anything at the fair we laughed and said well you've got some tough competition with that Metal band. Martin shook his head and said whatever. though our laughter we heard yelling like someone was scalding a Kid and it was brutal. I looked up and about 25 feet away was Amir. His Dad was laying into him. Telling him how much of a disgrace he was and told him we were sent here for a reason so why disobey. He kept saying that over and over again. Eventually I had enough and decided to step in front of him.

The man said who the hell are you dumb jack ass. I yelled back I'm the guy who brought your son home when he got beat up in that parking lot and who read him when he was starving that night too because it seems like you haven't been feeding him much hell the poor kid looks like a twig. I was furious. The man pushed me aside and said to his son, ``This is the man you snuck away from home to tell lies to about your brothers. He then stick his finger in my chest. And said your people let Russia invade our country in the 80's and then we responded and instead of understanding the message you waged war against us and your soldiers killed even the innocent. Don't you see.

My face turned red as a cherry and a rage boiled inside me and I needed it with anger. then I yelled right into his ear you call 9/11 a proper response Mother Fucker raising my fist ready to fight. He pushed me. I yanked his shirt, threw him into a potty and said this town is not going to act kindly to that so you best be quiet. He yelled with his hand in the air, free to say what I felt. Martin and Jazz then began to pull me back as to have the last word I yelled and part of America is treating your kids with respect not as dogs. He chuckled and said whatever crazy White man. Martin then yanked me, turned me around and pushed me the other direction and said he's not worth it. I decided to calm down and walk away still perplexed by his ridiculous claims. We got to the car and got inside perplexed.

We closed the doors and everyone took a sigh of relief. We all said my goodness. A few minutes went by as we sat in the car with my wife, my friend and his wife. We sat there deep inside. They just wouldn't miss a huge argument between me and a stranger. I knew Amir but I hadn't grasped exactly what he had gone through in his daily life. He had a father who was pressing him into something he didn't believe in nor did he stand for and I didn't know what to do. I wanted to be a mentor to this kid but I wasn't sure how to tippy toe around the situation.

We then drove to the Bowling alley to witness one of the best small concerts ever.

Chapter 17

The Concert

As we pulled up to the bowling alley. The place was on fire not literally but figuratively. There was a huge crowd out front. Couple dozen teenagers just mingling. As you looked upon the place you could see a very large bowling pin encapsulated in neon. It was one of those signs that moved on a timer it would be facing straight up and the next light would have it falling down. The parking lot was well lit with large light poles with extended shades.

We parked our Car and piled out. When we got inside. To the far left is 10 lanes of bowling and to the far right is a small roller rink about half the size of a normal rink but it served our community just as well. And in the corner there are a few arcade games. In another corner there was a small kitchen and dining area. But front and center was a stage with two drum sets if you guitars tucked behind the stage Bright lights hanging from the ceiling. And everything was ready to go. Martin's first show and I was really proud of the guy he had told me that he'd been rapping for years and finally this would be his chance to show at least this town what it was made of.

It was about 6:30 so there was still 30 minutes of Time to kill. Martin had to get a few things set up so we let him be. So the other three of us decided why not bowl a game. And order a couple of sodas. So while I grabbed the bowling shoes and paid for the lane jazz and Kelli grabbed our drinks. I went up to the counter and asked the gentleman his name was Timothy as it said on his polo shirt. For three pairs of shoes and then asked him to reserve Lane four.

He gave me a nod and said that would be $13 sir I nodded back and said all right then. He then asked what sizes would you like. I politely said I wear a size 8 but I'm not sure about my wife and her friend. I then shuffled over to where they were standing then politely asked what shoe size do you guys have. Kelli said oh I'm a size 6 in men's because they never seem to carry women's shoes here. Been jazz said oh you should know this by now I'm a size 4 men's. I exclaimed oh that's right and then when I'm on my way back to the counter turned to look behind my back telling them to get me a Sprite.

I handed the man the money and told them the shoe size that I needed. Then I made my way to the lanes. We typed our names in a little system computer that they have that's super glitchy and old, And then started our game. I was up first. Me being a little bit brash and confident smiled at them and said watch this. They giggled and said well whatever. I had the ball in hand and spun it hard. The ball made its way down the track of wood then there was a crash as it connected with the first pin it knocked down six pins which I couldn't complain was not too bad. I rolled another ball picking up another three pins and hadn't got the spare but I was happy with it.

Both the girls then rolled their balls both picking up their spare. I was behind 10 to 9 and they were tied. A few frames went by six to be exact Jazz had about 46 points Kelli 39 points and I was stuck with the measly 30 points I've been pulling terribly the whole game and needed to pull out the last four frames to have any chance of winning. I was up and I decided I need to be focused or I just roll another terrible roll and end up the ball in the gutter. I breathed in and out a few times and then surely confidently flowed my ball down the lane. It had a good spin and it was online to meet with the very first pin it crashed and every pin fell. I screamed yes, throwing my fist in the air. Ask the girls cheered now that's how it's done, maybe you'll catch up with us. I said well I hope so.

The next few moments went by and I picked up my spares on each of them. But I still needed to get two strikes in a row to have any chance of winning as the girls were pretty good at bowling, something I didn't know as they both picked up their spares. Jazz was next up. She threw her arm into the ball and it flung down the way but it veered to the left and went into the gutter. She pouted a little bit then laughed.

Kelli then stood up and made her way to the front she picked up her ball and flung it down the lane. The lane is pretty Dead set but only knocked down about four pins. She then rolled it down the lane again and again and only knocked down four pins. The score now is 98 for Kelli 105 for jazz and I had only 82 points. If I got two strikes in a row I would beat jazz. And she was always the type to say don't let me win so I wasn't going to. I picked up my ball and made my way to the Lane and flung it down on the wood. It spun hard and fast and then slammed into the first pin and knocked everything down. I then nodded back at them and then said one down one to go. Jazz smiled and said well I guess so. I then waited a few seconds for my ball to come back. Then grabbed it out of the ball returner then flung it down the lane again. It slammed into a few pins and then spun into another few pins as it feared to the left and as it seemed I was going to get another strike as the last pin was balancing left and right and out of nowhere like a force field had just come upon it.

It finally settled straight up and it hadn't fallen. I slapped myself in my forehead and said well y'all win I had just barely lost. I had 99 points as the first loser but I was okay with it because as I turned I heard the music start. It was a cool hip hop beat and then I heard Martin start singing rap lyrics. I started nodding along thinking all right here we go let's see how he does. He started getting more intense with every word he said. He was intensely confident and I knew he was ready for the moment. Me and the girls made our way to the stage. When we got front and center there had been a few stragglers along the way that stopped to listen to the music. At this point Martin was really starting to get into it; he was rapping fast and right on point. He had plenty of emphasis. It was his if this is what he was made for. And I guess a few people from outside could hear it too.

A few moments went by and towards the end of his first song a bunch of people from outside had gathered up front to listen to him sing. Everyone was dancing and every few lines he would sing people would go ooh and ah catching the cleverness in his lyrics. A few minutes went by. And people are really starting to get excited one guy even hopped on stage. Martin just welcomed him like it was no big deal they started hyping each other up. He asked us all to start jumping around. After a few minutes the place was getting super Wild and I was pretty excited for my friend.

It felt like you really were starting to get a fan base right here at this moment after years of hard work with nothing to show for it. It was all paying off right here. He sang a few more songs with the same intensity. Then he decided to slow everything down. He sat down at a piano. He gave a big gasp into the mic and said here goes nothing. He began to sing a ballad. It was about his wife and how far they had come and where they were now. It was about all the things they had gone through in their life and also their relationship. They'd been together since high school and his dad was an alcoholic and her mom was a recovering drug addict.

So they shared a similar background and he was singing about that. And then he's saying about how they were starting a family and now they were going to do it differently. The end of the song came as soon as it started people were in awe I was too I just seen my good friend look like he was on top of the world he was in his element he was in his happy place it was like he was singing to a million people at the Grammy's or at a big live show but the reality was he was in front of maybe 45 teenagers and a few middle-aged men that were there to drink a few beers and then just his friends but in my mind I knew this was just the start. That was the end of his show. People cheered as he walked down the stairs of the stage. I looked him dead in the eye and I said this is only the start of this isn't it you're going to take this somewhere.

As we walked out of the bowling alley people walked up to him and told him how good he was and how inspiring he truly was and they were right. This guy inspired me to be a better man, to be a good husband and to work hard for what I do. It inspired me to take the leap of faith to be Amir's mentor no matter what came my way in that. I knew a lot of people would look at me wrong and misunderstand the situation. I knew it would be hard to do this given that his family would not approve. But in my mind I knew this kid needed a friend and that someone needed to listen to him so from that moment on I decided that my goal was to help this kid belong.

Chapter 18
A Million Little Pieces

That next morning I got up a little bit early. Jazz was still sleeping next to me so I gave her a kiss on the cheek and got up and went on to work. When I got there Denver told me hey some dishes weren't done last night do you mind taking them on. I said no biggie I'll be right on it.

I threw my apron over my head and made my way to the back of the restaurant. When I got to the dishes it was more than just a few dishes it was about 20 plates and 15 bowls some are really dirty and almost every bit of silverware I knew of in that whole entire diner. I was livid but I knew I'd still get paid for it so it wasn't a big deal. I started scrubbing along scrubbing my life away pretty much it was only my third day back since Ray had died and every once in awhile I would yell out his name say hey Ray look what's going on over here sometimes I'd see how dirty the pantry was other times I'd be looking into our walk-in freezer and see that there was a box of chicken knocked down or something like that and then I remember oh he's gone.

This time I yelled hey Ray want to help me with these dishes. Then loneliness would come upon me like it did before. I stood there thinking to myself I would never see my best friend again and he never be there for the little things like this but I knew in my heart of hearts he was in a better place and he'd want me to meet and there someday so my whole goal in life needed to be to follow my Lord and Savior like I hadn't been for a long time and to help the hopeless like Amir. And that's what brought my focus back to the same thought I had thought about the night before after the concert. I wondered where he would be after school.

I thought to myself what is he really going through at home. He's told me the little things and how his brothers treated him sometimes but until last night at the fair I hadn't seen the gravity of the situation yet and I still didn't know how to fully help this kid. It wasn't like I could call DCS or anything like that that wouldn't help at all, probably just make the situation worse. In my eyes it would really just feel like a betrayal. So I defied the plan that I would call him after work and go for a ride and just try my best to take him under my wing. The day went on like normal. There was a new waiter. She was from Wisconsin and had just moved to town.

She wasn't quite that good at her job yet but we gave her some Grace even though she messed up about 20 orders that day. When she wrote down fries they were supposed to be sweet potato fries. When she wrote down a classic burger and needed cheese little things like that. They're trying to get Martin to do Ray's old job but he wasn't quite catching on and I honestly understood being thrown into something like that so fast and also knowing who you are replacing can affect you too. It was a fairly busy day at the diner, always about 20 people or more inside, sometimes even more. Towards the end of my shift Debra asked me to take the trash out.

When I got outside there was Amir just standing there with a sad look on his face. I looked up and said hey kid are you all right. He said no after that crap you pulled last night my dad beat me and you put me in a worse situation than I was before. You should have just left it all alone. I could have taken care of it. I hate you. I said wait wait I was trying to stand up for you I was trying to help you. I was scared for your life dude don't you see that I didn't know what he was going to do to you and I was hoping that by standing up for you he'd start to see that things don't work like that in America like they do overseas where you're from that you have to respect your kids not treat them like animals.

Amir looked up he was enraged and I didn't understand why he said you don't understand anything do you you don't understand my culture. You just try to get me to conform you try to get my family to conform just like everybody else in this town why can't we have our own way I understand what you're trying to do sir my dad has his ways too even if I don't like them I respect them but no one else in this town seems to understand that no one in this town respects my family and even when I don't understand what they're doing and why I still respect them. I still understand why they do what they do but no one else seems to hear them out. So why do you think our people resorted to violence back in the day? I don't agree with it but now I understand because you Americans never listen. I understand what my dad says now. I then looked and said son I just don't want you being hurt I don't want to betray you that's not what I meant to do. He then snapped back then why didn't you stay out of the way you knew that was no good you should have helped me from the sidelines or something like that like those jocks or whatever they're called talk about. But no you step in front of my father and disrespect him like it's no big deal well it's a big deal because where I'm from that's something you don't do. Deborah then stepped out from the back door.

She looked at me and said now what's taking you so long. I looked over and said oh it's nothing, some kid just looking for food. She said well he can't get any he'll have to pay for it. Amir instantly threw his hands up and started cursing in Arabic. Debra said well let's get inside before this kid gets irate with us Then we both went inside. I was super upset and kind of guilty that I just shrugged off a kid I really cared about like it was no big deal. I had betrayed him now I have pushed him off to the wayside and treated him as nothing. After the small bond we had made that just that morning I was hoping to build had now just been shattered to a million pieces.

Chapter 19

Wisdom

For the rest of my shift that day I felt terrible. It affected me so much I was messing up orders. All I wanted to do is clock out and find Amir and try to fix our friendship. The end of my shift finally came and I finally was able to clock out. I texted him and told him to meet me on his street corner. He texted back responding fine. I then made my way to Korr street. When I got there he was sitting on the stop sign Pole. I yelled out hey kid we need to talk real quick. He got up, I opened the door for him and he stepped in. He gave me a really dirty look. I looked him in the eyes and said kid I'm just trying to help you. I then said I apologize for the other night. I know it affected you in a negative way and I should have just stayed my balance and talked to you about it later.

He looked at me and said it doesn't change the way that I'm treated now and what I have to do. I asked him what do you mean what I have to do?" He said I have to live in this hell with my parents and my brothers. And I have to take

71

on their pain that they cost around town. With the things they say to people and how they act so no matter what I do I get their blame and I guess I deserve it. I looked at him and said no you don't you didn't make these decisions. You looked back and said you are forced to make decisions if I'm being honest it is who I am on the inside. I might not say insensive things like they do but it's in my blood. I said kid you're a good person no matter what anyone says to you keep that in your heart that you're a good person and you're not what everyone says you are. Amir then looked at me and said well are you working this weekend. I said very much that if a football team wins the championship game that place will be bumping the next day it'll be everybody in this town there so yeah I'm working. He looked at me deep in my eyes and said well I'll see you there. I said okay see you then said if you need anything I got you kid 100 %. He got out of his car and slammed the door. I than asked him cuz I had noticed it before I said why do you smell like gasoline dude. He looked back and said I had to fill my dad's gas tank in his car and spilled some on myself. I said oh okay I'll see you later. He looked back and said you bet you I'll see you Saturday night.

The high school football team had won all their games and were playing for the state championship game that Friday. And if they won there would be a massive party at the diner that next night. Sadly I had to work that day but we were definitely going to play it on the radio. But anyway after I saw Amir get to his house I turned the car around and made my way home. I felt better about the situation with me and the kid. I feel like I could be a mentor to him which he needed. He had all the kids around town telling him how terrible he was and how his family was a disgrace. And then he had his family feeding them all these lies.

I knew that somewhere in himself he knew that he was a good person and that all I needed to do is show him that was true. So I drove home. As I pulled into the driveway there was jazz smiling and waving a little bit more pregnant now as it had been almost 2 months. She had Pedialyte in her hand and looked kind of tired. I pulled the keys out of the ignition and got out of the car. She asked if I thought you got off at 4:00. It's almost 5:30 now. What were you doing? Oh you remember that kid from the fair the other day that I stood up for. Oh yeah I remember that how could I forget you almost killed his dad. Well I ran into him and we talked. I tried to clear things up and it went well. Just said well that's good how was your day at work. I looked over and shook my head. It went all right, a little bit of a busy day but nothing too crazy like the normal flipping burgers and trying to go as fast as I can trying to get out of there to see you. She then asks how's Denver doing with his leg and everything. And then shook my head again. He's doing all right, not too bad he's got the cast and everything off but you can tell he's still stumbling around a little bit and it's never going to be the same. Jazz then looked up again and said is it weird without Ray there. I shrugged of course it's weird when you're best friends not there anymore I'm lucky they have Martin there we joke a little bit and feels always coming in kind of almost to the end of my shift and we get to talk a little bit. And Zoe just got a new job so she's working two jobs now working at one of those hotels on the edge of town and then at the diner she was telling me how that was going just doing pretty good just cleaning a few rooms and running the front office on the weekends. Well tell me about Phil, how is he doing I haven't talked to him in a while. He's doing just fine. He's proud of his kids playing in the state championship game this weekend. You know he's Phil deep voice and all that. She then said I just got off the phone with Kelli. I said oh yeah how's your pregnancy going. She's doing okay throwing up everyday but can't say any different for myself.

I then asked have you heard from Grandma lately ?" I've been busy and haven't been able to visit him. She called me about 3 days ago. He was doing okay. His breathing is more shallow lately and she's probably got a few months left in him but he's still alert enough to talk. You know you should probably go visit him today. I said yeah I guess so do you want to go with me I'll go in about 2 hours spend a few hours with them and come home and sleep. Jazz obliged. I think that would be great, she said. All right, well we'll cook some dinner, watch a TV show and we'll go see him. All right then sweetie what do you want for dinner. Chicken soup sounds really good. Okay I'll get a few cans made. I took my jacket off as fall was turning the winter and it was getting colder and colder outside but we still hadn't got our first snow storm which I was sure was coming just around the corner.

I sat down and flipped the TV switch on. I flipped the channel 140 ESPN Aaron Rodgers had just passed for 600 yd the night before on Monday night Football. And Serena Williams was preparing for the next tennis season. Tiger woods was finally coming back from that car wreck that you've been in months before. And Drew Brees was thinking about coming out of retirement to play for the broncos. After the food was made Jazz came into the living room with a few bowls she said can we watch something else.

I grunted and said okay okay what would you like to watch. She said how about the office. So I plugged our laptop into the PC port on the TV and went to Netflix and started watching the office. It was that one episode where they were trying to catch the bat and Dwight was doing all types of crazy stuff. We watched about two episodes, then I looked down at my watch and it was almost 7:00. I looked over to Jazz and said all right let's go see Grandpa she nodded her head all right. I threw my jacket back and helped her up from your chair. She handed me the keys and we made our way out the door. Hopped in the car and started driving down Henderson Lane. My grandpa lived about 15 minutes just outside of town.

The phone rang. It was my grandmother so I answered the phone and I said hey Grandma I'm actually on the way to your house there was a long pause I said Grandma what's wrong what's wrong. She said well you better hurry to say goodbye to your grandpa. The hospice lady told me he probably won't make it through the night. I stomped on my brakes and pulled to the side of the road. So I wouldn't do anything horrific. Jazz said what the hell are you doing. I looked over to her. Tears flowing from my eyes. She was enlightened instantly to what was going on. She grabbed the phone and put it up to her ear and she embraced me. She said it's Jazz. Can you tell me what's going on? And then she also burst into tears. We sat there for a few minutes on the side of the road crying hysterically. The car was just idling. After a few minutes I came to my senses and said we best get going.

We were now about 5 minutes from my grandpa's house. We pulled up to the driveway and both of us got out frantically. Grandma had also informed my mom and she pulled into the driveway just a moment later. We made our way to the door. Grandma had tears in her eyes and a few feet away we can see Grandpa laying in his hospital bed motionless pretty much in a coma. A week ago I thought he was going to be okay for the next few months so I took it for granted and now I am thinking that that's why you are so jealous of us and here's the moaning and just says I wish I could have that.

We all sat down at the kitchen table which wasn't very far from Grandpa's bed. It was a very small house, two bedrooms, one bath, very small kitchen, very small everything pretty much besides the big garage in the back my Grandpa would work on his cars and his motorcycle. But anyway we sat there and she offered us some food but all of us just said no we're okay we all just ate not too long ago. I looked over to my mother and she had some tears in her eyes. I said Mom it's going to be okay, he's going to be in a better place tomorrow just like you told me with Ray they're both going to be sitting up there together Happy's as always no more pain no more suffering no more dealing with this illness.

She shook her head a little bit frantically trying to say okay but couldn't because her anxiety was overcoming her. I grabbed her head and pulled it into my chest. A moment went by and then we all decided to gather around him. My grandma prayed over him and kissed his hand and his forehead and told a story about how they had a picnic when they were young and he spilled all the wine on her favorite blanket and had to explain that to her dad that night they were only 17 then she with tears in her eyes started to laugh and looked up at us and said it's going to be okay we'll see him soon. Next was my mother. She kneels down and put her head on his chest, tears still flowing from her eyes. She gained her composure and started to say hey Daddy it's all going to be okay we love you and you raised me well and you help me with my kid and you became his dad when all those unfortunate events happened in our life I'm so thankful for you you mean the world to me thank you for helping me with all that homework when I was a kid doing my hair even though you had no idea what you were doing and being the best friend that I needed every moment that mattered.

Jazz then came forward and she looked down and hugged my mom and started talking to him she said hey Gramps you were like a father in a lot of me you always had good advice and truly cared about me like nobody else you are a good man and there's no doubt that we'll see you in heaven again. I stepped in and Jazz cleared the area I kneeled down next to my grandpa and as I began to talk he kind of woke up. I said hey Grandpa you don't have to wake up just rest. He said, ``No son, I want to have a conversation with you for the last time. He said son you've got a lot coming up in your life you've got a kid coming you got all those bills you're working good at your job and I'm proud of you but always remember this do the right thing even when it doesn't seem like it counts even when no one else would do the same and have a relationship with Jesus don't worry about religion keep your eyes on the Lord and love people no matter what. Even when everyone would do the opposite thing, make the decision to put others first even when they hurt you, do that in your marriage, do that in your friendships and do that with your enemies.

I love you grandson and I'll see you soon again. With that he closed his eyes and peacefully passed away. We all huddled together for a few minutes praying and mourning our loss my grandmother Louise then called the ambulance a few minutes later they came and took him away. I called into work for the next day and spent some time with my grandmother. Denver offered me the week off but I declined.

I told him you're going to need me on Saturday and I'll be okay, just give me the rest of this week until Friday and I'll be there. Denver said I guess so kid if you need a week off don't even call me I'll understand. We spent that Wednesday and Thursday planning a funeral for my grandfather. We got to the morgue to prepare his body. We all wrote our eulogies and contacted family friends of ours and rented it out of church for that next Tuesday afternoon. We were all sad but also happy as always. The thing was we all felt at peace because we knew my grandfather was okay, he was a good man and we knew where he was, he was gliding through heaven right there with Ray. In myself I knew life was never going to be the same I just lost my best friend and now my grandfather and almost 10 years ago my own father I had lost a lot of important people in my life but I knew if I leaned on my family well what was left of it and my friends and what was left with that I would be okay.

Chapter 20

A Joyful Frequency

It was a Friday morning, it wasn't just any Friday morning it was the Friday morning for the state championship game. Though I had graduated almost 5 years ago I felt just like a high schooler again. The town was full of noise every street littered with glue bend high School gear big trucks driving up and down the main roads with flags representing the school. In just 12 hours they would start the game. They'd be leaving for Bismarck at noon and the game would start at 6:30.

I would have gone to the game but I was working the late night shift and I'd be working till about 11:30. There wouldn't be that many people around town before the people that were going to be there. They'd probably be in the diner for the listening party. That's everyone that got off work too late to go so I knew there would be at least 50 people gathering there listening to the game on the radio. Around 11:00 I still have 3 hours to my shift started so I decided to head to the high school to see the boys on their way there was a large crowd of about 500 people all settled in ready to wave to the boys as they got out of the bus and half an hour and bye and we saw all the kids making her no way on the bus the cheerleaders walked by and made their way onto their bus.

The buses pulled away as they did that burst of air came out pashhh sound that you hear as a bus pulls away. Everyone cheered, glue bend glue bend glue bend. A tale of cars followed the buses. It was mostly parents and plenty of students that said let's ditch school today and go hang out with our buddies. The crowd began to clear about 20 minutes later so I hopped in my car and made my way to the diner. I got there about an hour before my shift started so me and Denver decided what the heck let's eat some lunch. He made us two plates of hash browns and biscuits and gravy. He said how's the wife I responded to. She's doing pretty good. Her pregnancy is going well and well besides my grandpa dying we're all doing pretty great.

He said how about them boys making it all the way to state I remember when you guys were right there. I said I know right I'm proud of them I grew up with some of those kids and they worked hard to get where they're at. I then said what's your prediction on the game score and who's winning. He said Fargo's pretty damn good they only lost one game and it was out of state so they're undefeated in state too. They've won every single game by at least 30, something we can't boast about. And they won their last playoff game 50 to 10. We squeaked out with a 20 to 18 win so we're going to be having to play on the top of our game. And as for the score I'd say it's going to be pretty high scoring I say we win 38 to 31.

How do you think it's going to go you said. I looked up from my plate well I give them the win obviously as I'd hope and I guess I'd hope to see a defensive game other than I think it's probably going to be 21 to 20. Denver said well we'll see. We then talked about the NFL and how the NHL season was going and how North Dakota state was doing pretty darn good and their hockey season and their football season. Then we talked about next months company bowling tournament. Denver said well Phil one last year and I don't expect anything else. He pulled a 250 and everyone else Bowled about 150 so if we had any chance we were going to have to hit the bowling alley every single day to catch up to him. He just had a natural talent for it I guess.

30 minutes went by and it was time to work. Few hours went by and the place was pretty slow so I cleaned the fryers. They're pretty darn dirty so ask Martin to help me out a little bit. He tackled the grill is I squabbled with the fryers. We rolled the turkey meat and put it in its Cold Case Denver then asked me to check the beer fridge to make sure everything was organized I had to move a few cases of dos Equis around but it was no big deal. After about an hour the first Rush came in. It was about 4:00 and everyone was getting their meal before they hit the road for the game.

There were a lot of to go orders and we ended up running out of to go boxes. The grill was hot, burgers, chicken sandwiches and all types of different things were being made. After the place began to clear a little bit I helped Martin prep his fries for the next day we'd stick a potato in a slicer slice it measured out 8 oz then toss it in a bag for the next day. After about a half an hour of doing that we moved on to cleaning and doing dishes. There's about 200 plates in about 400 cups that needed to be cleaned. I won't bore you with that cuz you know how that is once we got the dishes done and some of the cleaning done we hosed off the back loading dock.

At this point it was around 6:00. Denver came to the kitchen and said hey boys take a break. So that's what we did. Me and Martin sat down and had some dinner and talked about life. I invited him to my Grandpa's funeral and he gave me his condolences. We then talked about how his brother was selling his car and how I should buy it because mine was a piece of garbage and we needed a nice car to bring our kid in home with. The game just started right after we got off break. The radio was blaring throughout the kitchen and everyone who hadn't gone to the game was starting to come into the restaurant. Glue bend was kicking it off to start.

They kicked it off. Fargo's returner was able to return it all the way to the 40 yard line. They then ran their first play from scrimmage and was able to get a 7-yard game from a run. On the second play they threw a deep ball and one of the Glue bend safeties dived and batted away from the wide receiver. On the next play however Fargo's running back ran all the way to the 8 yard line. We were able to make a goal line stand in Fargo to settle for a field goal. The announcer said I think this might be a pretty good game. Lots of big plays and stops in the red zone will turn out to be a nice one. We'll see how it goes when the other announcer peeped in.

There was about 9 minutes left in the first quarter when Fargo kicked it off to glue bend. A returner grabbed it and then fell over as he got hit underneath his legs. We made a few nice plays throwing a deep ball 20 yd and running for another 30 but then Fargo put the brakes on the drive and we ended up having to punt from the 50 yard line which they ran back to the 50 yard line. Fargo then threw an interception to replace later which gave us really good field position at about the 12 yard line. We ran a few run plays to no avail. It was fourth down and our coach had a decision: did you want to tie the game or try to get lucky. He decided to go for it but it didn't work. They threw the ball and a wide receiver caught it. It was hit right away just two yards away from the first down. When Fargo got the ball back they threw a deep ball which resulted in a touchdown. When we got the ball back we put a good drive together with plenty of run plays melting the clock away but we weren't able to get into the end zone so we settled for a field goal. The second quarter is more the same us playing good defense then playing good defense and US settling for field goals. At the end of the second quarter it was 13 to 9 Fargo had the lead. like I had thought it was going to be a defensive grudge match.

As we could hear the halftime festivities start over the radio, I decided to take a break. We made ourselves some sandwiches and gathered with a few other people that are hanging out in the diner. Mr Denson, a slender 75-year-old man, walked up to our booth. He said what a game is only going to do now to score a touchdown. Martin looked up and said I know right I think they got a real good shot at playing good defense and the crowds behind him. There were a few songs that played on the radio and then after about 15 minutes the second half was about to start.

Denver sat next to us as we're about to stand up. He looked over to Deborah and said turn it all the way up we're closing the kitchen for the rest of the night. Drinks are on me, let's settle in for the rest of this game. The third corner is about to start. I called my wife and told her to get in here. Everyone isn't at the game right here. They've even shut down the diner. She said I'll be there in a minute. The announcer's voices came in through the radio a little bit fuzzy but clear enough to know that the second half kickoff was about to start. Fargo lined up the kick and booted it into the end zone. Glue bend would get the ball the 20 yard line.

Our quarterback huddled the boys, told them to play and shuffled them to the line. After barking a few commands he hiked the ball. He faked a quick hand turned and threw it about 5 yards up the field to his tight end. The tight end turned upfield spun off of the defender and then it was taken down a few yards short of the first down. On the next play the fullback took a hand off and ran for 8 yards. The offense put a few more run plays together just like that and then they faked the handoff and ran a screen pass to the left the receiver caught the ball and his blockers let him 42 yd all the way down to the five yard line. On first and goal they're in a dive play that got them three yards.

On the next play they threw a pass in the end zone that was batted down by Fargo's middle linebacker. It was now 3rd and goal. Glue Bend called a timeout. The coach was talking to the quarterback as the offensive coordinator talked to the rest of the team. They then went back on the field and huddled for a quarter of a second and then ran back to the line of scrimmage. As we are sitting in the diner the anticipation grew. The announcer said here we go, it's the moment of truth. Are they going to be able to get in the end zone today?

The quarterback hiked for the ball then began his five-step drop the offensive line broke and defenders started to rumble towards him with a quick decision he turned around and rolled out. He then found his half back wide open in the back of the end zone he flipped it up to him with a bit of a rainbow pass and at the edge between out of bounce and in bounce he caught the ball and fell down. Touchdown glue Bend touchdown glue Bend the announcers yelled. They then kicked the extra point.

On the next play they kicked it off to the other team and they ran all the way back to the 20 yard line of glue Bend. The defense stood their ground though and forced the field goal. The score now was tied at 16. The score stayed that way for the next 8 minutes. When Fargo finally kicked the field goal a long one too the 43 yard field goal which by my high school standards is pretty darn hard. But then glue Bend struck back with their own field goal. As we headed into the front stretch of the fourth quarter with about 5 minutes left it was tied 19-19. Fargo was getting the ball. It was kicked off and they ran it back to the 40-yard line. Their quarterback marched his men to the line and hiked the ball he threw it down the middle to his tight end who ran it all the way down to the 30 yard line.

They then went to draw play with their half back who ran it to the 25-yard line. I'm the very next play they took a strike to the end zone which was caught. They went for two but missed. The score now was 25 to 19. Everyone at the diner was a little bit hopeless thinking we were going to lose but had that little bit of Hope in them saying we can drive down the field and score a touchdown and kick an extra point. We did it once in this game and we can do it again. But on the kickoff the return of and Fargo returned it and then fell at the 8-yard line.

There were only 2 minutes and 15 seconds left so even if we got the ball back there was never going to be enough time for us to score a touchdown and then kick a field goal or score another touchdown. So now the only hope was a turnover. Fargo hiked the ball and ran into the outside. But their man was hit hard and hit the ground for a loss of two. On the next play they ran a flea flicker which is a play where you hand it off to the running back and then he pitches it back to the quarterback and then they throw it. As he threw it his player caught it he then turned trying to dive into the end zone and then it was smacked just shy.

Now it was 3rd and goal at the one yard line. We could hear the crowd roaring from each side. There were 59 seconds left on the clock. All they needed to do was knee the ball then kick the field goal and there'd be no chance for us to win. The quarterback lined his men up and victory formation. What that looks like is him standing under center in his full back and running back lined up directly behind him side by side. He hiked it and needed the ball. The seconds were taking off the clock. Then the glue bends coach called his last time out. There was only 15 seconds left on the clock and borrowing a miracle would be the only way to win. After that Fargo decided that they should kick the field goal and put the game out of reach. Everyone in the diner had their heads down knowing the game was pretty much over. We all looked at each other and said well we're proud of them. They had a beautifully Good Year. Can't ask for much more. They played really well against a really good team, a team that was blowing other teams out by 50 and we kept it within 9 they ought to be proud of themselves. Everyone in the diner nodded their head when Denver said that. Meanwhile in the game father was lining up for their field goal the ball was hiked but the snap was pretty wobbly. And the holder fumbled it. The kicker then haphazardly kicked it from off the ground as it was about to go through the back of the end zone for a missed field goal. Phil's son jumped up and grabbed it right out of the air. Even put his head down and ran as hard as he could juking out the fenders trying to find a way out of that end zone. The time was ticking there was only 12 seconds left. He shoved the defender to the ground with his arm out in front of him and then hurdled over another one he spun and then headed to the sideline.

The announcers on the radio we're struggling to keep up with where the ball was and what was going on. They were frantically asking each other what was going on. And then through a cloud of players. Then the announcers hollered. Connor Houston is running down the sideline. The diner exploded in joy. We could hear through all the commotion the announcers yelling he's at the 40 he's at the 30 he's at the 20 at the 10 at the 5 touchdown. We could hear the crowd through the radio roaring just as we were. The boys of glue bend had just Won State. The Diner would be a roaring place Tomorrow. I looked over to Denver and we both said are you ready. Both knowing just about everybody in the town would be at the diner tomorrow.

Chapter 21

The Diner Down
The Road

I woke up it was Saturday morning as you already know the high school football team I just want to state championship and I was getting ready for work I'd be going in at 12:00 that day and working till close I was reading myself for the party they would start at 6:00 and most likely and at closing time. I was a happy camper when I opened my eyes that morning. I looked over to my wife, almost two and a half months pregnant. She was a fast asleep pregnancy pillow under her back. I raised my arms to do my morning stretch as always and let out a big yawn. It was going to be a happy day. I threw my work uniform on then sat down on the couch. At about 10:00 in the morning I had at least an hour and a half before I would need to start driving to work. So I turned on the TV and flipped through the channels looking for something to watch. All over the local news channel said blue Bend won the state championship last night with a close game versus Fargo sure to be a party tonight see you there at Denver's Diner 6:00 Sharp. I chuckled under my breath what a work day it's going to be for me I thought to myself. I finally settled in to watch some ESPN. Then I flipped on Netflix and watched the office for a few.

I looked at my phone after a while. It was 11:45. I have 15 minutes to be at work. I got up and grabbed my keys. Jazz was just waking up. She walked out in her pajamas in a low-cut shirt. She looked up and smiled then did a shuffling type of stretch as she walked. I welcomed her to sit down next to me. She said babe you've got like 15 minutes before you need to be at work let me give you a kiss and I'll see you tonight 6:00 Sharp I could hear you blaring the TV all the time then she laughed. She gave me a kiss on the cheek and then on the lips. Then grab my coat and saw me out the door. I got on my way as I was driving to work. I saw Amir walking along the road. I slowed down a little bit and yelled out my window hey kid do you need to be somewhere.

He yelled back at me to be sure if I can get a ride to the supermarket that would be great. I pulled the door open and invited them in. I gotta go quick but I'll get you there.

I asked him how he was doing. He said well things aren't the best at home but I'll see you at the diner tonight I said all right you bet. 2 minutes later I dropped him off and just 5 minutes later I was at work.

I slammed my car door shut and ran up the loading

dock into the back of the restaurant. Martin and Denver were hooking up a few breakfasts for a few guests that we had had. I greeted them. Hey guys, how's it going? Are you ready for the party? They looked back at me and nodded. Zoe came around from the corner and bumped into me. She said oh Josh I'm sorry how are you doing. I nodded my head and said I'm doing pretty good. How about you? She said I'm doing quite fine today feeling fresh and ready to go. One of our new servers Ashley came up to the cooks' counters and yelled out two cheeseburgers one with bacon one with jalapeno both with a side of potato salad. A few minutes later Denver gathered us all for a meeting. He said hey guys we're expected to have about 400 people in here at any time starting at 6:00 and ending at 12:00 it's going to be a long day guys I'm calling in all the troops just know I got your back all day and we're going to have a great day and celebrate that big win and we had last night you guys ready. We all shook our heads and said I think we'll manage as long as we have all 20 of us that work here and help we should be just fine. Denver then spoke up and oh I've got some good news some of the people over at the grocery store told us if we start running out of food just to come pick it up. He then looked over at me so Josh that's going to be your job today and once we start running out of stuff I'm going to have you run over there and fill up your whole entire car and come back that's probably going to happen twice all right.

I agreed with him and it sounds like a plan I exclaimed.

Then said all right, guys we're going to have a free up and down day until we get to 6:00. Try to save your energy and let's have a great day. We then all went back to our tasks. Phil came into the restaurant at about 3:00 and he and Martin started prepping every single thing you would think of, even stuff that we usually don't prep. While I made pies and sliced bread and did everything I could to prepare for the neck wrenching day that was ahead. The place was pretty slow most of the day. I figured everyone was waiting for that night to come in and have their meal and celebrate the big win so it made sense. We may be sold 15 hamburgers and a few breakfasts that day.

I kept the grill clean and everything stocked up. Everyone was working hard and I could see as Denver walked around he was proud of us all and he was ready for a big day. At about 4:00 a few people started coming in wave my wave it was the early birds that decided they wanted to save their seat. Denver head bought a couple of those Rubbermaid tables and chairs just to have some extra seating in the diner so not many people would have to wait outside.

At about 5:30 the head coach and a few of the players from the football team brought in the trophy. We said it went on a big circular table covered in confetti. We then started decorating certain parts of the restaurant with banners that said state champs and congratulations. Then soon enough the crowd began to get larger and larger. 250 people or so make their way from the parking lot to the restaurant. They were even parking up on the hill. Where I parked it on the day of that flood a few months ago. The football players were all lined up on one table, about 30 of them. All with their leatherman's jackets on big smiles on their faces, a few with scars from the night before. As the people came in, the orders also came in. Plenty of burgers and lots of pie, especially chicken pot pie. A couple steak dinners. It was a pretty busy night so far after about an hour it got even busier there were about 600 people All stockpiled into this medium sized Diner. We are starting to run out of food. So Denver told me hey go get that food from the grocery store. I nodded my head. I'll be right back. I made my way to the car.

On the way there I saw this black van just sitting in the parking lot. It seemed kind of odd. I'd never seen it before but anyway I just went on with my business. I was wondering where Amir was. He told me he'd be there at least 7:00. And it was almost 7:30 and I hadn't seen any of them yet. I picked up my phone and texted him hey buddy where you haven't seen you yet at the diner. He texted back I'll see you soon buddy 30 minutes or so and I'll be there. I then texted my wife telling her that I picked her up right after I was done at the grocery store. I pulled up to the store and they were waiting for me. They loaded me up with fries and burgers, lettuce, tomato steaks and all sorts of things. And then scattered along to my house Jazz was waiting outside. I popped the door open and she hopped inside.

As we drove along it started to snow for the first time. Just flurries nothing much. As we pulled into the parking lot we could see there were even more people. I looked over to Jazz, kissed her on the cheek and said I'll make sure you get a seat. My mom and my grandma are in there towards the back of the restaurant. I shuffled inside and waved down to help me with the groceries. We started unloading bringing things to the back of the restaurant. A few of the waiters and waitresses were helping us put it into the fridges and pans that we needed to. As I looked upon the dining room there had to have been at least 700 people. The most people I've ever seen in that place. Even the backup seating that we had put in place was starting to run out. People were standing next to each other. When I looked into the kitchen I could see that the dishes were just piled up. We had started just using paper plates knowing it was no use.

The crowd of people talking was very loud and roaring every time one of the waiters would put in an order they'd be screaming at the top of their lungs. As I was making a burger Denver looked over to me and said dude this is crazy. Remember that day back in August where we made like $20,000 in a day and I thought that was the biggest day we've ever had. Well, we've tripled that in just 2 hours. Few minutes went by and the head coach called a toast fork tapping against glasses, even some Solo cups but what do you expect when there are so many people you're going to start running out of glass cups. But anyway the coach stood up and began to give a speech. We stand here today victorious and never lost a game. If you would have told me that at the beginning of the season I would have laughed. Two days honestly looked like foolishness. But as soon as we got that first game under our belt confidence bloomed and hard work instilled itself in every bone of this team we put our heads down and played hard. There wasn't a single kid on this team that did not put their blood on the line. I remember a game must have been our fifth game one of our wide receivers right here sitting next to me his name is Tony he ran a route and when the ball was throwing to him he got hit right away squished between two defenders and it was a catch that put us in a field goal range and we wouldn't have won the game without him he shouldn't have caught the ball but he did. We didn't think he was going to get up, we thought you took a licking. Just before I was going to call the time out you stumbled up and then called the field goal unit on and blocked for them too. When it got to the sidelines as we had just won the game he said to the coach I was never going to let you down, never you work so hard for us I'm going to work so hard for you. At that moment I knew our team was destined no matter what.

The diner began to whistle and shout and clap. I even joined in dealing with a few whistles of my own. The quarterback Eric Riker then stood up. He began to speak when I started my high school career. I was this tiny little kid 5 ft 2 110 lb. They didn't know where to put me. I didn't even know if I would survive. Coach just said well let's see if this kid has an arm. They handed me a ball and I just threw it 40 yd. He looked at me and said son you put on some way to build some muscle you got potential and I will be there for you the whole way through. And that's exactly what he did. I sat on the bench a lot my freshman year. My sophomore year came I was second string I struggle a little bit so they moved me to third string but then when both of the quarterbacks got hurt I had to step up and I didn't do that well but we squeaked into the playoffs in the first round we lost 50 to 12 I threw four interceptions and it was truly my fault. As I sat there defeated, the whole team surrounded me and they comforted me. They said that you got us the field goal four times against the best team in the state. What else can we expect you to show determination and he never gave up, you never laid down. My junior year just last year we started the season 0 and 3. We had to win every single game or we were going to miss the playoffs. The coach sat me down and he said son I know you can do this. We've lost every game by two points literally every like two points. Now we just got to get one out. The next game is a road game and I slept on that field and I said there's no way I'm going to let this team lose. With 2 minutes left in the 4th quarter we were down two and we had to start that drive from the four yard line. The kid looked around at his teammates they all remembered. He then went on. I threw the ball a couple times and missed and it was fourth down.

He then looked over to his teammate Thomas who was a fullback. Thomas here looked over at me in the huddle and just said I got you I'm open. On the next play I hit him and he ran for 45 yards. And the ball a few times and then on 4th and goal I threw into the back of the end zone and it was a touchdown.

From there on out I had finally had the confidence and it wasn't because of me it was because my teammates believed in me. Trusted me and had my back and if it wasn't for that moment and even though we didn't even make the playoffs that year that one moment of trust and determination gave me and my teammates the chance to do this and be where we are today state champs I am thankful for every teammate and every commuting member every cook in this restaurant everyone that believed in us all here I think you will you guys all helped us get here.

Everyone started to chant Glue bend Glue bend. Everyone sat down and the commotion went on. More burgers we're getting ordered and I was getting overwhelmed so I decided to take a bit of a break. I looked over to Denver. He was making some burgers with me. I said hey buddy I need to sit outside for a minute to get a breather. He nodded at me all right buddy I'll give you five minutes. I said thanks man see you in five. I walked out on the loading dock and sat on the ramp. After a few minutes I heard some pops very loud like fireworks. I wondered what it was. I figured maybe someone was heading out and wanted to celebrate a little bit but I didn't see anything in the air I wondered huh whatever. I headed back inside when I got in there I couldn't see anybody standing there was no noise and I was really confused. No one was talking. Denver wasn't cooking burgers. I started looking around and that's when I saw Phil shot in the arm he was leaning against Denver's door to his office. He had his finger to his mouth motioning me to be quiet. I whispered what the hell's going on dude what happened. He said some dudes in masks came in here and just started shooting. Coach got shot in the chest and he's gone. I said do you know about what happened to your family?" He said my kid I think he's dead and my wife I think she's under a table.

The popping started again pow pow pow pow pow. Everyone started to scream. There was a lot of scrambling, people started flooding back towards me in the kitchen and people were rushing out of the front doors. And every once in a while someone would hit the ground. And then within a matter of 30 seconds it got quiet again. At this point I decided that I needed to drag Phil somewhere safe and hide. So that's what I did. I dragged them back into the freezers. I knew it would be really cold but it's better than dying. I pulled out my phone and dialed 911. I told the operator I can't talk but just listened. I stuck my phone out of the door. There was more popping and gunshots firing then it was a loud boom. It was the smell of gasoline and metallic and gunpowder like a bomb had gone off.

I decided I needed to investigate. I picked my head out the door of the fridge. That's when I saw that the front exit was engulfed in flames. The only way out was the back and I knew it was only a matter of time that whoever was doing this was going to come hunting for me. I looked back at Phil. He had a terrified look on his face. He asked me what we do man I'm wounded and we got all these people to help I'm not leaving man until I find my wife. I looked back at him and said I don't know what to do. I started to army crawl back to the grill. I saw one of the gunmen ranging back and forth back and forth almost like you was patrolling.

It must have seemed like he didn't know I was there. He probably thought that we all rushed out the back or that we were all shot. The guy was about 6 ft 2 and gloves on his hands couldn't tell what ethnicity he was. And since he was just patrolling the back I knew there was more than one guy. I texted Amir and told him do not come to the diner there's been a shooting. He instantly texted back hahaha we got you now you're here we'll find you. I shook my head. It couldn't be, he was part of this he couldn't be doing this. Then it hit me that he and his family had been sent here to just wreak terror as I remembered how at the fair his dad kept saying we were sent here for one reason and this was the reason.

A few minutes went by and the bomb went off. As I peek behind the counter I saw bodies piled on top of bodies. The state championship trophy was now melted into a football player's body. But I could also see a few people still moving and somehow alive, basically clinging to it at this point. I didn't know what to do but I knew I had to take these guys out. The police were at least 15 minutes away. I looked over to Phil and motioned him over. As I did the gunman looked back and fired a bullet striking him in the leg but the gunman couldn't figure out where he exactly was so he was free. I looked around what can we defend ourselves with I thought to myself. The only thing within arms reach was a spatula and the temperature gauge. I slowly reach my hand for the temperature gauge that has a sharp edge. It wasn't much but it might help it was my only chance. I started to crouch creeping along the side. I told Phil are you willing to be a distraction. he said well how, I told him just grown a little bit it will turn him away and then I'll stab him in the back.

So he got himself as far back in the kitchen as he could and then started to cry out and the gunman looked back and said where are you you're done now. I crouched along the side and I got up and lunged stabbing a gunman right in the back. The temperature gauge went straight through his back and out through his neck he started to bleed uncontrollably. I then dragged them by his feet. Out of the corner of my eye I saw Martin motionless in the corner. I stumbled over to him. I shook his body and checked his pulse. He was cleaning his life. Then all the sudden he opened his eyes and said Josh help me. Help me. I don't want to die my wife's already died. I looked out into the crowd of people in there and Kelli was all burnt up motionless. I looked over to him and said she might be okay, she'll be okay. I was lying to myself and lying to him. I just wanted him to have some hope and I hope that that wasn't the same fate for my own wife.

I prayed silently that Jazz was okay. I couldn't live without her. I then told Martin I can't move you anywhere or we're going to get seen acting like a possum dude. Chuckled a little bit his blood rushed out of his mouth I guess so dude this is terrifying. I ran back to where Phil was and the wounded gunman. Who was now gasping for life. I pulled his mask off and said who are you and why are you doing this. I looked into his eyes. It was one of Amir's Brothers. I shook my hand.

Why kid why. As he let out his last breath he said allahu Akbar. I said shit a terrorist attack in North Dakota. Phil looked up to me and said you've got to be kidding me just saw my own son take a bullet for his mother. My other son made it out thank God my two littlest we're with their babysitter tonight. We sat there for a few minutes. Another pipe bomb went off and glass broke from the booths. I peered my head around the corner hoping I wouldn't be shot instantly. I saw three more shooters. One was wounded and One of which I knew was Amir knowing in himself that he didn't want to be a part of this. He was a good kid in the wrong situation in the wrong hands. And I knew also I was going to have to kill him or he was going to kill me. I then ran back into the kitchen. I looked over to Phil and he said what did you see?" I said all right we got three shooters we took out one we got to take out three. He began to look around. All right all we got is a Bunch of knives man that ain't going to serve us much bringing a knife to a gunfight fuck man what are we going to do.

He said what if we go to the back door and just get the hell out of here and run and let the cops take care of this. I said well we could do that let me check. I looked through the people and there was a massive fire. I said dude that ain't happening they set a bomb off back there. The blazing gun fire went off again and again. I went down on my knees hoping it wouldn't hit me. I screamed out oh my God. Phil like fuck it dude we got to find a weapon. I said we got this gun and Whatever ammo is left in it we got to use it. He said all right let me use it, you take some knives. I said all right and then I looked down and there was a pan of boiling Grease. I pointed down on it. He shook his head then whispered you pour that on one of them take the knife out of your pocket stab the other one and i'll shoot the last one. All right that's the plan then.

We both stood up. He brought the butt of the gun to his shoulder. And we charged out to the front of the. Gunshots started to ring out bullets flying around our heads. Feel aimed at one of the guys and shot him in the knee but it wasn't enough to bring him all the way down.

Me looking like a crazy man had the boiling Grease sitting on my shoulder and it's pan. I threw it straight out and one of the gunmen landed right into his head. He screamed out in tears. I then retrieved the knife out of my pocket and went for a man's throat. It sliced right through his trachea and he fell straight back. Blood gushed from his throat as he gagged. The next gunman fired a few shots at Phil hitting him in the stomach three times and then they both ran out of ammo.

The last gunman started to chase me. I got back into the kitchen and we pretty much started to play tag as I bobbed and weaved through the kitchen. Out of the corner of my eye I saw him lunch at me. I grabbed him by the arm and threw him on the grill. I started pounding him like it was an MMA fight elbows to the face, he grabbed me by the throat and pulled me in close. He grabbed my arm and threw it right on the grill, burning my tee shirt off and boiled my back. I Screamed out in pain. He started yelling at me he had my whole body up against this grill you wonder who robbed those hotels who burned those fields that was my family were wreaking havoc. I didn't say you son of a bitch trying to ruin our town. I flipped the envelope on him. I grabbed his leg and tipped him over onto the fryers his body laid over top of them. I knew I had to end this. I needed to stick his head straight into them. I began to grab his face as he struggled. I managed to stick his hair in his scalp into the friars. I tried to tip his legs back but he was struggling too much with me. He would grab my shirt in my arms and karate chop me on my hands.

All of a sudden my grandfather's voice came over me to do the right thing, do the right thing even when no one else would do it. Love God and love people even when it doesn't make sense. I then threw him on the ground and laid on him. Then ripped his mask off. It was Amir. I said kid why you're a good dude it doesn't make sense why'd you try to kill me I love you man. He said I come from a torn family. I am nothing to nobody I said you're something to me you mean something to me man I'm going to help you get out of this I'll talk to the police and tell him the situation and I'll take you in like my own son. You don't have to face this anymore. You deserve to be a kid again, you deserve a new start.

I then brought him to his feet. I told him I need to detain you. I got to stick you in the fridge for a minute man. He nodded his head all right. That's the least you can do after sticking my head into a fryer. I laughed a little bit and he did too. As I locked them in the freezer I said it's all going to be alright dude I'm going to figure this out. I walked out to the kitchen to see all the Carnage that it happened music was still in the air at this point for some reason The sound of silence came over the speaker I looked around baffled but what I saw all of a sudden I saw my mother laying there motionless I kneeled at her feet next to her was my grandmother completely torn apart I began to cry a little bit but I knew she was with my grandfather now.

I tried to wake my mother but it was no use. I yelled at Jazz's name. It seemed like she wasn't there. I looked around. Miss Johnson had a bullet straight through her head coach that completely destroyed bullets in his chest and back everywhere half the football players were laying on the ground dead. My neighbor David gone also. I then stumbled into the bathroom to wash my hands of the blood. That's when I heard a girl shuddering. I swung up in the small door and it was my wife. She yelled out not knowing it was me don't touch me. I then embraced her jazz Jazz. It's okay. It's me. we were able to kill them. It's all going to be okay.

We laid there crying for a few minutes. She said did you see Mom and Grandma they're gone I was just barely able to get myself in here he was no way out. I said yeah half the town is dead is about 200 bodies out there. Martin's wife died and martins barely hanging on to life. She then cried out again why. It's over now baby, it's going to be okay. I told her to stay here. I've still got one of the gunmen in the freezer and he's unpredictable. She asked who is he. I looked in the eyes and I told her you're not going to believe me it was Amir. She said no way I said yeah remember when his dad kept saying we were brought here for one reason remember him saying that at the fair right before I confronted him well that was the reason to kill everybody in this town for no reason.

I then called back the 911 operator. I said how far are you guys we've neutralized the situation but I've got about wounded and 200 casualties. They said we're about 2 minutes out. I said well you guys need to hurry. I got three people clinging to life and I'm the only person that's not wounded. I then sat down next to my mother and began to cry. I weeped and weeped. The sound of silence still played in the background. I heard the sirens ringing in the background.

I went to the freezer and pulled a mirror from there I walked him out the back door we're police officers were about 30 ft away I said it's okay it's okay this guy was forced to do this I yelled and yelled but they didn't listen gunfire went off in a mirror fell to the ground split his head open they hadn't shot him in the head but shot him in the knee when he hit the ground I knew he was dead. I hit the ground and said why he's an innocent kid he was forced to do this he was miss informed and forced to kill. I passed out about 2 days later I woke up in the hospital.

Jazz was sitting right there. She told me his reporters were outside asking for you but I told him there's no way you talk to them. They're saying you and Phil are some type of heroes Phil skipped town. He has no reason to be here now his whole family died. Martin's a mess I'm a mess and soon you'll be a mess. I looked up at her and said I want to talk to those reporters and I'm only going to say one thing. She said are you crazy? What do you want to say. I cleared my throat, you'll see I explained. Bring one camera in one reporter. A Few minutes later they came in. The blonde haired reporter say for yourself sir saving your town from a terrorist attack. I looked dead into the camera. I am no hero, not at all I only killed just like those terrorists did. And guess what one of those shooters I knew well he was my friend I was his mentor he was a young kid 15 and definitely a good kid too. In a rough family that forced him to do this and when I brought him out to the cops they didn't ask any questions they shot him. Now don't get me wrong they were doing their job and I'm not trying to stir up any racial divide but he was innocent if he didn't do this he was going to die. Just like everybody else. I loved this kid. I treated him like my own son. He had a beautiful smile, an appetite like a dog and he was kind. Amir was his name he had compassion, did not judge people and loved the people around him whether they loved him back, But now we sit here one more life lost in this tragic day.

I then looked at the reporter and said get out of my face. The next few weeks were rough. We had to plan more funerals. My friends were in shambles, those that were left of them even survivors guilt set in like a train wreck I know for a fact if I was inside when it started I would have died. Denver was shot and he tried to escape; he didn't make it, his wife didn't either. No one knew what was going to happen to the diner; the mayor had been shot also. A few weeks later I visited my grandpa's grave. I said you were right to do the right thing even if no one would do it. Then it snapped inside my head. My whole entire family besides me and my grandfather had died by gunfire. There had to have been a reason for this.

My God wanted them there for a reason. When it's your time it's your time that's something my grandfather always said to me. Now I know what that reason is because 7 months later a new kid was on the block and he was mine. 7 pound 2 ounce Luke JR named after my grandfather. O was grateful to still have my life and the new wisdom I carried. I write this story on my deathbed. My life is coming to a close but well for my son his has only begun I'm sure you'll here his story one day but for now much love and hope to all and One last thing before I go. Let me tell you a diner isn't just a diner it's where family start when two lovers meet each other on their first date. It's where families grow. It's where friendships are made. It's where memories are built, and I almost forgot GO GLUE BEND ROCKETS.

Chapter 22

Epilogue

I feel like in our society these days we point the finger at every other nation in all nationalities for all the problems. If you are white you blame African Americans for all the violence and the other way around. When there is a War going on all we do is blame the other side. Even Hitler had his reasons. He felt that the treaty of Versailles was so unfair that he had to do anything in his power to make his nation all powerful. This goes very much the same for Isis and many other groups of their kind. Even after 911 when we went to war with them our soldiers did the same things to civilians turning them against us. Nowadays, good law abiding Muslims are looked at as killers who only are looking for bloodshed. When you see someone that serves a different God than you don't look at them funny don't think that they're a terrorist. There are bad people in the world but that very same person could be a very good person, a person that makes you smile that could change your life. So let's stop killing each other and find common ground. It's simple: there are good people and there are bad people. There is love and peace and than there is haste and bitterness.

CHAPTER 23

DEDICATION

I dedicate this to my boss at the wing shop and the bakery. I dedicate this to all of my coworkers who inspired a few different characters in this story and encouraged me to keep writing. I would like to thank my wife for not letting me stop writing. She encouraged me and was very happy for me. I had always wanted to write a book but didn't know how. I would also like to dedicate this book to my mom and dad who believed in me from a young age that even though I have dyslexia and quite literally cannot read very well, I still knew I had the potential to do this. I Would like to thank Mrs. Dougan, my dyslexia tutor who brought me so far. If it wasn't for her I would've never made it here todayI would also like to thank Tom Fox, my professor who gave me the tools to understand what I was doing. I would like to thank my editors who are probably going to edit these very words that I am writing. But I also like to think of Miss Gores and Mr Ro.berts my English teachers in high school, for always refining my work and giving me the tools to write. I would like to thank my grandfather who I literally formed Josh's grandfather's struggles with cancer into this book. I would also like to thank every veteran who fights on the front lines for my life who fights the bad guys in this story in real life. Last but not least I would like to thank Bobby Hall otherwise known as logic for inspiring me to write this book through your novels and memoir to show me that I am capable of doing the same.

Printed in the United States
by Baker & Taylor Publisher Services